C. P. BOYKO

NOVELISTS

stories

BIBLIOASIS
WINDSOR, ONTARIO

FIRST EDITION

Library and Archives Canada Cataloguing in Publication

Boyko, Craig, author
          Novelists / written by C.P. Boyko.

Short stories.
Issued in print and electronic formats.
ISBN 978-1-927428-71-9 (pbk.).--ISBN 978-1-927428-72-6 (epub)

          I. Title.

PS8603.O9962N69 2014   C813'.6   C2013-907287-X
                                                C2013-907288-8

Edited by Dan Wells
Copy-edited by Zachariah Wells
Typeset by Chris Andrechek
Cover designed by Gordon Robertson

Biblioasis acknowledges the ongoing financial support of the Government of Canada through the Canada Council for the Arts, Canadian Heritage, the Canada Book Fund; and the Government of Ontario through the Ontario Arts Council.

Versions of these stories have appeared in *PRISM International, Witness, Confrontation, CNQ: Canadian Notes and Queries* and *The New England Review.*

PRINTED AND BOUND IN CANADA

CONTENTS

For Bertie
And for Andrew, who lowered our rent

THE WORD "GENIUS"

MR. MALCOLM GAWFLER could not sit still. He was alarmed, though he did not know why. Something terrible was about to happen, but he did not know what. War? Famine? An earthquake? Yes, that would be just his luck: an earthquake the same day his new book was launched! A gaping chasm would swallow up all fifteen hundred copies, he supposed. In any case, survivors of earthquakes did not run out the next morning to buy new novels, but instead useful trash like bandages, food, and rope. Yet he was expected to perform tonight, to read aloud passages of this scandalously irrelevant work, as if an apocalypse were not hanging over his head! He had another cup of coffee, to steady his nerves, then another; but for some reason, this did not help.

Mrs. Deirdre Gawfler watched him sadly as he lunged about the room, muttering and making gestures of hypothesis, decision, and renunciation. She intervened long enough to straighten his cuffs and wipe the ever-present smut from his fingers. His large, knobby hands were trembling and his eyes were wide open, as if to Injustice.

"You'll do fine," she said, though she knew better, and patted his lapels.

"Who cares?" he cried, tearing his arms free and throwing the cuffs again out of alignment. He felt like a man going over a waterfall being reassured that his hair was well parted. "Who the deuce *cares?*" He clutched his chest and resumed pacing.

Sometimes Mrs. Gawfler wished (for his sake) that her husband were not a novelist, but something less taxing, like a priest, or a soldier, or a prison warden.

But she needn't have worried about that evening. The reading was a success, at least compared with previous occasions. In the past, Malcolm's nervousness had filled his speech with long, bewildered pauses; it was as if he had never seen his text before, did not recognize the language it was written in, or indeed the alphabet. That night, however, he read derisively and incredulously, like an angry atheist mocking the Bible in church. This new style was deemed by the audience an improvement. It was certainly quicker, and got the drinks served sooner. Mrs. Gawfler noted with relief that Lady Astmore had complied with her private suggestion and withheld coffee.

An hour later, when Mr. Gawfler had more or less subsided to his normal level of excitability, Mrs. Gawfler made her excuses ("The children …") and took her leave. On the way out she touched the arm of Mullens, the publisher, to remind him of the little matter of the book reviews.

Mr. Gawfler, meanwhile, was feeling more optimistic. He no longer felt that an earthquake was imminent, or even inevitable. Probably the people in this room would live to ripe old ages. They certainly deserved to. They were good people, intelligent people, with obviously refined tastes. They deserved to be happy. He toasted them, individually and collectively, with the latest in a series of whiskies that had begun mysteriously to appear in his hand. He did not normally like whisky—he did not normally drink—but this stuff, really, was not half bad. He could give credit where credit was due. Tears came to his eyes at this realization of his own generosity. His epitaph, he thought, might someday say, "Kind Even To Whisky." Cigarettes too. He did not normally smoke, but at one point in the evening someone offered him a cigarette—or anyway allowed the hand holding it to drift too near his gaze—and Mr. Gawfler plucked it from their fingers. He sucked on the thing as if trying to draw a pebble through it; when his lungs and cheeks were full, he threw back his head, puckered his lips, and exhaled a magisterial cloud of dense white smoke. A moment later he was seized by a fit of hacking, shuddering coughs. When the worst of these had passed, he looked around him, dazed. "Where did *that* come from?" he wondered.

All but two of the people in attendance were known to him personally, and these two were promptly recommended to him as the rarities they were. The first was a man who claimed to have read all his books, and, in proof, quoted a few lines that he had particularly admired—and which Mr. Gawfler did not recognize at all. The feeling that came over him whenever one of his friends strayed from generic into specific praise came over him now. He felt stiff and uncomfortable and fraudulent. All that old stuff seemed so far behind him! Why did no one ever praise the paragraphs he'd written that morning, for instance, or the ones he was going to write tomorrow? The little man before him had a receding upper lip, caterpillar eyebrows, and squirrel-tail side whiskers. Mr. Gawfler thanked him, delivered some thoughts on the indispensability of the reader in the creative act, and autographed for him a fresh copy of the new novel (thus obligating the poor man to purchase a second one). Then he turned his attention, by turning his body, aside.

The second stranger was a woman who also claimed to have read all his books. She made other claims, too, some of which were not comprehensible to Mr. Gawfler in his exalted state, and many of which were interrupted by Mr. Gawfler's own enthusiastic agreement. She claimed that his characters really lived; that he had a remarkable understanding of women; that she would rank him among the preeminent novelists of the day, alongside Mrs. Humphry Ward and Mr. Jerome K. Jerome; that she had read *The Layman and Lord Newbotham* three times, and that "that Newbotham" was a "real subtle character"; that his use of punctuation in the Laura chapter of *Mrs. Dreazle* was simply extraordinary; that one sensed such sadness beneath the bright pageantry of his plots; that that bit about birds and trees at the end of *Jebediah Stokes* was perhaps the finest piece of really lyrical prose since she didn't know when; that she loved his inventiveness, his compassion, his sense of humor; that she loved his mind. She had a protruding lower lip, a drooping eyelid, and a chin like a spade. She spoke with a modulating inflection, as if her voice were an instrument she was trying to tune. She sounded always on the verge of breaking into embarrassed laughter. Mr. Gawfler was charmed. He spoke with her, to the exclusion of everyone else, for the rest of the evening. He did not even think to sign for her a copy of the new novel—an oversight which would have significant consequences, as the reader shall presently see.

Mr. Gawfler was not what one might call a good sleeper. He did not sleep easily, and especially did not fall asleep easily. He seemed never able to get all his many long limbs inside the bed at once, but had to fold and refold himself this way and that, tucking parts of himself away wherever they would fit, as if his body were one too many towels to be stuffed into a drawer. He was always too cold or too hot, a difficulty rendered quite unresolvable by the possible combinations of seven blankets and the window's several hundred possible degrees of openness. And in addition to these physical discomforts, he had to contend with a restless mind ... Consequently, he often leapt into bed at the first yawn or telltale sign of mental fogginess, hoping to smuggle himself across the border into the Land of Nod while his mind was off its guard, as it were. But inevitably, as soon as his head hit the pillow, acute mental clarity and crackling wakefulness lit the inside of his brain like a searchlight and he found himself, against his will, pondering such questions as how many bees it took to make a teaspoonful of honey, whether or not Reverend McAdams would like the books he had lent him, what funny things the children had said at supper time, whether or not he had brushed his teeth, whether or not he had that morning used a semicolon incorrectly, and *how long* it would take so many bees to make so much honey. When he realized that his mind had tricked him and that it had no intention of turning off, he became angry—which of course only woke him more fully. But his anger also made him more determined, so that he would often lie there for hours, his eyes clamped defiantly shut, his every muscle straining with the effort to sleep.

That night, however, he sank into his vast mattress as if it were sun-warmed moss; his limbs unfolded effortlessly and imperceptibly, like petals unfurling in springtime; his joints exuded a pleasant healing fatigue, like cut branches exuding sap; his eyelids were warm stones; waves of happy accomplishment flowed down his spine; and his mind hummed in wordless contentment, like the final dying notes of a symphony. His last thoughts were: "Mrs. Brewler; her name is

Mrs. Brewler," and, "She loves my mind!" Then the luke-warm tide of slumber came in and gently extinguished these last embers of consciousness.

But when the morning came, something was wrong. He awoke convinced that all his anxiety of the previous after-noon had been justified—that something terrible had hap-pened after all. He lifted his head from the pillow (it was like shifting a sack of meal) and looked hard at the world. He found signs of the catastrophe everywhere, in every thing: the way his shoes lay empty and abandoned on the floor; the way all that remained of yesterday's coffee were cold dregs; the way the very walls were blistered and peel-ing, as though bursting with rot. He sloshed himself quea-sily upright and stared out the window. The sun glazed the hills of mud with a harsh, tacky, amber light, like syrup that had congealed. There had been no earthquake, perhaps, but it would have been better if there had. He staggered out of bed, and armed with nothing but a terrific headache and a tongue like a slab of cold turkey wrapped in a handkerchief, he launched himself out into the world to find the cause of this cataclysm.

Mr. Gawfler, you see, was an intellectual, and had, as I have endeavored to show, the intellectual's tendency to become bewildered by his internal, emotional states, and the intellectual's need to find rational, external explanations for them. In short: He felt bad, and he wanted to know why.

He had not far to seek. The smell of frying rashers reached him on the stairs, and he realized that their cook was a sadist. The page boy passed him in the hall and tipped his hat, and Mr. Gawfler realized that they employed the most incompe-tent, lazy, and insolent help in the world. In the dining room his children lunged at him like feral dogs and wiped their sticky paws and muzzles on his pyjamas, and he realized that parenthood is a prison sentence. His wife said "Good morning," and he realized that he hated her.

Ah, God! It hadn't always been thus. He'd loved her once. He'd even *been in love* with her once! An image opened in his mind like an old wound, a vision of the fields outside Hawksmoor where they had rambled that summer, so many years ago. Ah, God, the cruel ravages of time! thought Mr. Gawfler poignantly. He'd been in love then, certainly—though he may not have realized it at first. He thought he was just being gentlemanly, keeping the poor girl company. He explained his happiness, when he recognized it as happiness, as the logical result of so much exercise, sunshine, good conversation, and, yes, feminine beauty. For he had to admit that her hair in the sunlight looked as soft and thick as a muskrat's pelt, and he did rather like the way her little pouchy cheeks framed her mouth like parentheses when she smiled, and he supposed he admired the way she moved so easily, like a single swath of fabric wafted by a breeze. But he also found that his nerves jangled, his extremities tingled, and his insides became muck in her presence. He concluded that she had an abrasive personality.

He required nearly two weeks to achieve insight. The day before he was due to return to Fulfordton, he called at his aunt's a few minutes early—and discovered that Deirdre sat on the floor like a child to tie her shoelaces. Then, while they were walking, she mispronounced a word: she said that Blake was too "eth-real" for her. These idiosyncrasies warmed his heart almost painfully; he did not know why. He believed he was embarrassed for her. In fact, she was endearing herself to him.

An hour later, he finally understood. They had found and venturesomely reclaimed an overgrown trail through a hedge of blackthorn that led down to a secluded bower where a stream gurgled complacently, like bathwater draining from a tub. The natural sanctity of the setting, or perhaps the thought of his imminent departure, rendered the two of them mute. Eventually he noticed that, every minute or so, and quite unnecessarily, she smoothed back the hair from her cheek with the last two fingers of her hand. Fear coursed through him; his blood tolled like a bell with the realization that she was nervous in his company—that she loved him.

And so, at last, he was able to see, in the mirror of her feelings, his own.

"Would you," he said, "will you," he said, "would you by any chance like for me to—permit me to—read you a chapter or two of my novel?"

He remembered how her eyes had shone with emotion.

Yet it was all doomed to end here, at this awful table, with these horrible, still-quivering strips of fried pigflesh on the plate before him!

Still, there was no use denying it: he had been happy once—ah, God!—happier than he had been at any time since.

Until, that was, last night.

He brooded over his breakfast, clutching his fork and knife like bludgeons, and occasionally making strictly defensive attacks on his rashers. He managed to keep them at bay; but his thoughts were another matter.

Why should he have been happy last night? What about last night could have made him feel so good, so much better than he had felt since he was in love?

His rashers enjoyed a momentary respite as his utensils fell still. Everything became clear.

Mrs. Brewler's face, certain characteristics of her voice, and even a few of her words came back to him. He realized—that he was in love.

Mrs. Gawfler watched her husband throw down his utensils, stagger back from the table as if warding off a blow, and galumph out of the dining room without a word. She listened to him trudge upstairs to the attic, grapple with the door for a moment before slamming it vindictively shut, and begin resolutely to pace—setting out each time, from alternate corners, with renewed purpose, as if determined *this* time not to be checked. She smiled, sighed, and raised her eyebrows all at once. It was always something of a relief when Malcolm returned to work after a long hiatus—even though in many ways he was more difficult to live with when he was writing. He began to sleep at odd hours or not at all; he forgot to eat and to shave and to wash; he became irritable and preternaturally sensitive to all "noise" and "clutter"— two fluid categories which seemed to encompass, at one time or another, the set of all things audible and visible. Thus it became necessary for the cook to prepare only "quiet" meals, bland foods which could be ingested with minimal distraction to the eye, ear, nose, or tongue; for the children to eat at other times or in other rooms; for the gardener to do all his work on the south side of the house either before dawn or after dusk; and for Mrs. Gawfler to do without house guests or callers for the four or five months Malcolm required to complete a book.

On the other hand, the hours when he locked himself in The Brown Study were her most productive. It was considerably easier to answer his correspondence, pay his bills, organize his library, and make a clean copy of the latest pages of his manuscript when he was not constantly buzzing around. Nevertheless, she knew that, relieved though she now was, in a month or two she would begin to miss him, begin almost to long for the day he would be finished—that first jubilant, attentive, loving day of idleness, when he would bundle her and the children outside for a romp in the fields or a long botanical walk through the woods. By all appearances he seemed to hate the writing life; but he needed to write, she supposed, so that he could occasionally feel by contrast the joys of not writing, of not having to write. Still, sometimes she wished he wrote short stories.

She sent the children outside with the nurse and both maids and luxuriated, for nearly five minutes, in the silence and freedom of solitude. Then she returned to the library and resumed her hunt through that morning's newspapers for any mention of her husband's new novel. Distantly and soothingly, like the ticking of an old grandfather clock or the dripping of a faucet, came the sound of the novelist's regular, agitated pacing.

But Mr. Gawfler, as the reader knows, was not hatching a new novel; he was reluctantly but with scrupulous honesty convincing himself that his deduction was correct—that he was indeed in love with Mrs. Brewler. Whenever his arguments lost coherence, flying apart into so many fragments of excitement and dismay, he dragged himself back to facts. It was true, at least, that she was in love with him. She had said as much—had she not? "I love your mind," she had said. But what was he if not his mind? To say "I love your mind" was to say "I love your soul," or "I love your *you*." So she loved him. She loved him! Panic swept through his body—and he assumed that this was reciprocation. He felt ill, and supposed that this was love.

He did not *want* to be in love—and with a married woman! He had not planned this; he had not asked for this. —Or had he? Mrs. Brewler had sensed a "sadness" behind his words; what could she have meant by that, if not a secret dissatisfaction, a hidden longing? She knew him better than he knew himself! He had never imagined that his books were autobiographical in any but the most superficial sense; but here was the counterproof. He went to his bookshelf and looked at the volumes he had so naively produced over the years. It was all there, unconsciously encoded in his books. He flung open *Mrs. Dreazle* to the celebrated Laura chapter and read at random: "For surely, thought Laura, Mr. Edmunds would not—would he—dare to presume...?" Good God! He snapped the book shut in amazement. He had never once given conscious thought to the expressiveness of punctuation, but that one sentence now struck him like a compact essay on the subject. Those dithering dashes, that pregnant ellipsis, the excruciating uncertainty of that question mark! He pulled down *Jebediah Stokes*, opened to the last chapter and read: "The hawthorns were in full bloom..."—and could read no more. At one time, he would have been hard-pressed to define "lyrical" prose, but now he could do better: he could point to a quintessential sample of the stuff! Finally he tore into *The Layman and Lord Newbotham*, where he found this: "Mr. Clarence, laboring under the misapprehension that his presence was still desired, crossed the room to the picture window." Mr. Gawfler, unable at first to grasp the Brewlerian significance of this passage, caught himself *reading it three times*. Then he riffled back and forth till the eponymous hero appeared, and he stood flabbergasted by the portrait of this monster of subtlety: "Lord Newbotham thought it better, for the moment, to say nothing."

Mr. Gawfler, for a moment, felt naked before Mrs. Brewler's clear and all-seeing gaze. She knew him inside and out; she knew every nook and cranny of his mind—and she loved it.

Did Deirdre love his mind? He supposed that he supposed she did. But his mind, he now realized, was in his books. Did she love his books? It had been years, surely, since she had given him any definite indication that she admired his work. Good God! Perhaps she *hated* his mind! Perhaps their entire marriage was, intellectually, a sham!

After five or six hours of further deliberation and five or six thousand false starts, Mr. Gawfler at last successfully hurled himself out the attic door and down the stairs, determined once and for all to wrench this matter into the open.

At the sound of his portentous tread on the stairs, Mrs. Gawfler signaled as prearranged to the nurse, who was to find the maid, who was to tell the cook to warm up Mr. Gawfler's supper. Mr. Gawfler, however, did not go to the dining room, but joined his wife in the library. He snapped his mouth open and shut a few times, then fell into a chair and began methodically rubbing his face and head, as if searching for something he had glued there for safekeeping. Mrs. Gawfler put away her writing things and gave him her attention; she sensed that he wanted to talk.

"Confound it," cried Mr. Gawfler at last. "What did you think of—" But at the last moment he balked, and named instead a colleague (or adversary) whose recent three-volume novel they had both read and which he had grudgingly enjoyed. Mrs. Gawfler replied vaguely and promptingly; but to her surprise, Mr. Gawfler did not take the bait. He wanted to know what *she* thought.

Mrs. Gawfler sat fully upright. It had been several years since her husband had read his day's work to her, but she remembered how trying it had been for them both. She genuinely liked his prose, but when she praised it he suspected her of humoring him. When she denied this, he questioned her objectivity. When she tried to oblige him by scraping up some helpful criticism, he accused her of caviling, and losing the forest in the trees. Unable to say the right thing, Mrs.

Gawfler had resolved to say nothing; and soon Mr. Gawfler stopped soliciting her opinion.

Now she sensed a trap. She had in fact liked Mr. Paulsen's novel, had been entertained and moved by it, but she was afraid that praise of another man's work might be construed by her husband in his present state (she was acutely aware that he had eaten nothing all day) as condemnation of his own. Pressed for comment, she said that she felt on the whole that it was rather unfortunate that the heroine had had to drown her baby at the end. By this she meant nothing more than that drowning one's baby was a sad event, something to be avoided whenever possible. She was even congratulating herself for hitting upon so unobjectionable a view, when Mr. Gawfler objected, and objected vociferously.

Mr. Gawfler, it must be remembered, was a novelist, and his approach to novels was that of a novelist. On the page, instead of people, some more, some less likeable, he saw characters, more or less believable; instead of stories, some more, some less engaging, he saw plots, more or less skillfully constructed. For him, all criticism and commentary referred to craftsmanship; he could understand no other possible attitude. But Mrs. Gawfler was essentially a reader; and while she was certainly capable of evaluating the artistry employed in the making of a fiction, this was not her usual method. Especially when a novel was good, she was content to take the people as people and the stories as a record of their lives.

So, this is what happened: Mrs. Gawfler said that it was unfortunate that the heroine had drowned her baby. Mr. Gawfler took this to mean that it was unfortunate that the *novelist* had seen fit to make the heroine drown her baby; that, in other words, this act was not credible, or was in some way not artistically proper. He argued that the heroine *could have done nothing else*—by which he meant, of course, that the novelist would have been wrong to make her do anything else; he thought the finale was fitting, and indeed beautifully tragic. Mrs. Gawfler, however, interpreted these statements not in the aesthetic sense in which they were intended, but in the moral sense with which she had opened the discussion; so it seemed to her that her husband was not far from saying that drowning babies was in and of itself a beautiful and fitting thing to do. She begged to disagree. And so the argument waxed heated, neither of its participants guessing that they were speaking at cross purposes, and both of them becoming more dogmatic as their antagonist became more outrageous—till Mrs. Gawfler seemed to Mr. Gawfler to be saying that one must never so much as introduce a baby or even a lake into a work of fiction, and Mr. Gawfler seemed to Mrs. Gawfler to be saying that all babies everywhere must be drowned always.

The contest was interrupted by the arrival of Mr. Gawfler's meal, which Mrs. Gawfler begged him to eat. Unfortunately, Mr. Gawfler did not know his own body as well as his wife did. (He had once consulted the local physician about what he feared were ulcer pains, but were in fact tactfully diagnosed as hunger pangs.) Taking his wife's appeal as a cowardly diversion or bribe, he swept the tray grandly to the floor and strode from the room, in dignified indignation. Back in the study, he nursed his newly shattered illusions till they grew into the conviction that his wife was a moron who hated his mind. This terrible truth gradually lodged itself physically in his abdomen, where a strange new feeling of aching emptiness began to consume him.

It was several days before Mr. Gawfler acted on this revelation. In the meantime, he became kindly, patient, and valedictory towards his family. At times he quailed at the drastic step he was about to take, and could almost believe that it would be better to let life continue in its old dreary course. But then the image of Mrs. Brewler—or rather, the image of himself that she had evoked that night—strengthened his resolve. He weighed the facts gravely and objectively, denying himself the sentimental luxury of modesty. If he had responsibilities to his family, he had even greater responsibilities to his Genius. (Mrs. Brewler had spoken much of Genius, and much of him; the implication was clear.) A man was put on this earth for some purpose; *his* was to write great novels. But could one write great novels, or any novels at all, in such a stifling, loveless, poisonous atmosphere as this? One could not. He owed it to his work, and to his readers of tomorrow, to escape before his afflatus was snuffed out entirely. Besides, an artist had an obligation to *live*, confound it!—to taste all that life had to offer. His *art* demanded that he love and be loved by Mrs. Brewler; let the consequences be hanged!

He worked some of these thoughts, discreetly and poetically condensed, into the telegram that he finally sent Mrs. Brewler later that week.

Thinking	much	our	conversation
forgot	sign	book	deepest
regrets	hope	sincerely	rectify
oversight	may	call	Gawfler

The response came in the form of a letter, effusive but brief, inviting him to call for lunch next Thursday. As per custom, this letter was opened, read, and replied to by Mrs. Gawfler, before being slid under her husband's door with the rest of the mail; so that Mrs. Brewler was rather bemused to receive two very different responses from the novelist. One regretted that a visit would not be possible as he was deeply immersed in a new novel; the other declared that he would be delighted to come. Since neither letter claimed to be a correction to the other, and since both arrived by the same post, Mrs. Brewler deliberated anxiously for some time over the guest list—ultimately striking an elegant balance between those people most likely to be impressed by an unexpected literary guest and those least likely to be disappointed by the appearance of no unexpected guest whatsoever.

The lunch proved to be not quite what the literary guest was expecting. To begin with, he was greeted at the door and divested of his inscribed novel by a short man with a driving manner and a head cocked to one side, as if he alone would succeed diagonally where all the timid, conventional world had failed vertically—and who turned out, in fact, to be Mr. Brewler. Something about the pointed brevity of Mrs. Brewler's letter had led Mr. Gawfler to believe that his was to have been a private meeting.

Having ascertained who, or anyway what, Mr. Gawfler was, Mr. Brewler took him around and thrust him upon the attention of assorted groups of his wife's guests. "A novelist," he said; then explained, "He writes novels." This fact never failed to meet with respectful astonishment, rather as if Mr. Gawfler had been introduced as an armless philanthropist who volunteered Sundays at the parish soup kitchen. Mr. Gawfler looked anxiously around for Mrs. Brewler as his new admirers asked him sensitive, probing questions about his work. Was it very wonderful being a novelist? Did he write in the morning, afternoon, or evening? How many pages did a novel have to be? So very many as that? Was it very difficult to come up with new stories and characters all the time? Would he put *them*—this lunch—into one of his novels? Was it very painful for him to kill one of his characters? Did he know Mrs. Humphry Ward very well? Mr. Gawfler was just beginning to resent the impersonal tone of these questions when someone asked him if he had been very devastated by the notice his book had received in last Saturday's *Review*.

Now, Mr. Gawfler, having published fifteen novels, had long ago cultivated a simple yet robust defense against book critics. He dismissed them all as fools. I would like to be able to say that this policy was not so self-serving as it may seem, for indeed Mr. Gawfler also applied it to favorable reviews; but the fact is that he did not receive many favorable reviews, and such as he did receive seemed to him thin, vague, and poorly written (though no more thin, vague, and poorly written than the bad reviews, let it be said). If he was hard on his detractors he was also hard on his supporters—because, in both cases, he secretly felt that he deserved better.

Mr. Gawfler implied something of this attitude in the frosty manner in which he confessed that he had not "bumped into" that particular review. Mr. Brewler (who owned part of a newspaper) was scandalized by this failure, as he saw it, of the national press to reach its intended audience; his head even shot upright for a moment. He resolved to rectify this minor collapse of civilization, and, tilting sideways with an intent air of peering right around to the dark backs of things, set out to find the elusive article. His determination was so manifest that conversation died and everyone stopped to watch, as they would have been compelled to stop and watch a man lift a house or wrestle a crocodile. He found his quarry on the sideboard; he ripped it from its hiding place, lifted it triumphantly over his head and shook it, as if to break its neck, and presented it to Mr. Gawfler.

Mr. Gawfler read the review. When he had finished, he laughed, once, as a fencing instructor in full armor might say to his student, "touché." But the fastidiousness with which he refolded the newspaper, making creases where none had existed, the new blankness that now entered his gaze, and the hollow joviality that entered his speech, betrayed something of his hurt—or would have, if Mrs. Brewler's guests had not found in these symptoms confirmation of their conception of The Novelist as a sort of benign lunatic, an absent-minded mystic with little interest in the mundane world of phenomena, little social skill, and even less sense of proper attire. The only thing missing was a filthy beard. They found him charming. The lunch was a great success.

Two hours later, Mr. Gawfler staggered out into the sunshine with a sick and heavy heart. "Those people!" he muttered. It was all he could muster for a time, so he repeated it. "Those ... *people!*" He decided he did not like those people. They were not his kind of people at all. They were—oh, dash it!—they were fools!

It had been a particularly bad review.

He walked to the train station with the slovenly gait of a child reporting for punishment. A carful of goggled motorists passed him in the road, sending a single small cloud of dust directly into his face. He stood there, sneezing and shaking both fists, for more time than it would be seemly for us to observe him ... Eventually his rage was distilled into thought: So that was what the world was coming to! A nightmare vision of the future appeared before him, of the earth weltering in a fog of dust and exhaust through which half-human holidaymakers, crazed with pleasure, blindly piloted expensive missiles ...

And the whole time, Mrs. Brewler had avoided him, maneuvering always to keep one of her guests between them, like a squirrel on the far side of a tree. He did not believe they had exchanged one word. And he had practically chucked his family over for her!

Ah, God, he was a fool. He did not deserve love, to love or to be loved. He did not deserve to experience things, did not deserve to taste even the most blighted of fruits from the Tree of Life. He was a scoundrel, a blackguard, a wastrel. He did not deserve to return home to his too loving wife, his too sweet children, his too comfortable chair, his too able cook, his too deferential page boy, his too industrious gardener... His mind rambled through his house and grounds with a heavy, sensuous self-pity, as if he were already a ghost there, who could look but never again touch.

That night Mr. Gawfler joined his family at the supper table. He sighed a great deal and ate whatever was put near him, but with an air of ponderous obedience, chewing long and swallowing each time with a shudder of revulsion. At one point David spilled a glass of milk on his father's sleeve, and there was a moment of exquisite tension; but Mr. Gawfler did not even look up, and merely muttered that it was no worse than he deserved.

Mrs. Gawfler was concerned. She had witnessed her husband's hopeful (if oddly clandestine) departure that morning and his lugubrious return that afternoon, and had concluded that the day's walk in the woods, where he sometimes did his thinking, had resulted in a setback. In the past, whenever he had decided that an idea for a novel had to be abandoned or radically reworked, there had followed a week or two of just this sort of dejection. She made a decision.

"Wait here," she said unnecessarily. "I've something to show you."

She returned with Sunday's *Spectator*, which she placed on the table beneath his dead gaze. Gradually, by fits and starts, the words on the page began to prick his awareness like so many pins and needles in a limb to which the feeling slowly returns.

He read the review. When he had finished, he laughed, once, as a bridegroom might say to his best man's toast, "Enough!" The elaborate nonchalance with which he refolded the newspaper, making creases where no newspaper had ever had them, betrayed something of his emotion. Soon he was on his feet and pacing around the table and tousling his children's hair.

"Dash my buttons!" he said at last. "That fool! That—*fool!* Where do you suppose he gets off? I mean really! It would make a cat laugh! Comparing me to Turgenev! I ask you!"

After a time his exclamations faded into bewildered chuckles. The nurse took the children upstairs for their bath and Mr. and Mrs. Gawfler retired to the library, where the page boy had already built up the fire. Mr. Gawfler placed himself in his chair and stretched himself to the full extent of his considerable length, running his hands over the arm-rests as if searching for imperfections.

"Of course it's all balderdash," he said gleefully. "Most critics after all are only failed novelists themselves, and trash is as often overpraised in its day as great works are derided and misunderstood and neglected in theirs. No, you can't put any stock in the judgement of critics. It's practically your duty to ignore them. After all, you don't want anyone else writing your books for you. Ultimately, you're the only one who can know if you're any good or not—"

He broke off, and his face crumpled slightly.

Mrs. Gawfler intervened. "Coffee, my dear?"

The doubt, whatever it was, passed. Mr. Gawfler smiled dreamily and nodded. A vision of the future came to him. He would drink much good, hot coffee. He would do much good, hard work. He would hone his mind till it was as sharp and clean as a stainless-steel instrument of dissection, and he would lay open the human heart in all its noble faltering, all its muddled glory. It was not for him to use the word "genius"; but someday he would be good, or even great. He would write a masterpiece yet to justify that poor silly man's praise—and that poor silly woman's. Perhaps someday he would buy a motor car.

SYMPATHETIC

HE DIDN'T RECOGNIZE her at first because she wasn't wearing her glasses; she didn't recognize him at first for the same reason.

"But it's you!" he cried.

They embraced, then pulled apart shyly, taking refuge in the scenery.

"Beautiful day, isn't it!" said Leora.

"Oh, very beautiful!," Alex agreed.

"Couldn't ask for better."

"Not this time of year."

"It *is* a bit windy, I suppose."

"That's true. A *bit* windy. But it's a good bright day at least."

"Oh, you can't fault its brightness."

"Although it *could* be clearer, I suppose."

"Yes. I like a few clouds, but this..."

"Yes. You might even call it overcast."

"I don't think that would be going too far."

"But at least it's nice and warm."

"No question about that. It's wonderfully warm."

"Though maybe there is just that slightest bit of a chill from time to time in the wind..."

"I wouldn't want to be out without a scarf and jacket, that's for sure."

"And yet," he sighed, "it *is* a day. There's no denying that."

"Oh indeed, it's a nice dayey day, if you know what I mean."

"We've that to be thankful for."

"Count your blessings."

They walked in happy silence for a while along the tar-black canal. The autumn's first rot was in the air, making the world smell almost fresh.

At last he said, "You've hardly changed at all, you know."

She swung her arms girlishly, so that the wedding band was visible. "I hope that's not true."

"You hope you have changed? Why?"

"I don't know. I suppose I don't care much for who I was."

After a pause he said, "I did."

"Well and what about you? Have you changed or haven't you?"

"*I* think so," he said sadly.

"Well then. Perhaps the new you will like the new me."

"As much as the old me liked the old you?"

"Isn't it possible?"

IT WAS AT THIS POINT in her thoughts that the novelist June Cottan ran over a little old lady with her car.

A startled, shriveled face appeared for an instant above the hood, there was a horrible polyphonic thud, June stamped on the brakes, and the car came to a halt—a more abrupt halt than her braking could account for. It was as if something had jammed the inner workings of the machine. June sat frozen in horror at what she had done, what she would find when she got out. Finally, with a shudder of resolve she threw herself out of and away from the vehicle, then looked back.

The car had completely swallowed the old woman's body; only her angry white head protruded from the gap between the front tire and the wheel well. June sank her fingernails into her mouth, cheeks, and eye sockets. She'd killed someone! She'd killed someone! She was a killer! She was—

When the old woman spoke, June fainted, briefly.

"Don't just stand there gawping, dummy! Fetch me my walker!"

Years of being ignored and flouted (as the old woman saw it) had honed Reginalda Drax's voice to a razor-edged implement for the extraction of compliance. June complied. All that remained of the walker, however, was a skein of metal projecting from the car's grille.

"I think it's broken."

"Broken my eye! You just don't know how to use it. Give it here!"

June didn't know what to do. Her scalp tingled, colors seemed brighter; the very street was suffused with momentousness. This *mattered*. But she didn't know what to do. She felt criminally remiss—as if this exact situation were one for which she should have prepared. Why had she never taken a first-aid course, for example? She dithered, flapping her arms helplessly and prancing in place, till Reginalda growled, "Give it here!" This was something June could do. She blew on her hands, planted her foot on the fender, and tugged at one of the twisted bars. When it came loose she staggered backwards—not realizing for a moment that the car had lurched too. It began to roll away downhill, gathering speed. June screamed and chased after it, without any idea what she would do if she caught it. The old woman's head rotated with the tire, smacking the pavement with each revolution. Reginalda, slightly confused by recent events, had the impression that she was being jostled. Loudly she muttered that people nowadays had forgotten what manners were. Then the car rolled into an intersection, causing several noisy collisions and partaking in several more.

June, breathless and sick with remorse, followed the convoy of ambulances to the hospital in a taxi.

JUNE COTTAN WAS A FUNDAMENTALLY cheerful person. That is, most days she felt happy, and when she did not, she felt it her duty to put on a happy face for the sake of others. When she took her dogs for walks, she waved at her neighbors and smiled kindly at strangers because she believed that other people were fundamentally cheerful too. When evidence to the contrary reached her in the form of a frown or a grumble, she chose to believe that these people were merely having a bad day—and her heart went out to them as she imagined in detail the sort of nasty rotten bad luck that could make you frown at someone who smiled at you. She smiled extra widely at these people, but with a wrinkle in her brow to show that she understood them.

For someone with as much capacity for sympathy as June, an emergency room is hell. It pained her to see so many nice people in such nasty condition. Few of them could or would return her smile; the wrinkle in her brow became a crease. One man had been waiting seven hours, and June's imagination saw him trudging through seven deserts in search of water. An old woman waited for her husband, and June's imagination flipped through the photo album of their happy years together, and she shared something of the woman's anxiety. One young man said to no one in particular that he didn't think he liked morphine, and June's bowels knotted in vicarious nausea. A pale girl with a band-aid on her thumb evoked in June's mind fountains of blood splashing a white kitchen. The sight of a healthy, cheerful-looking fat man caused her to shudder at the ant farm of decay that presumably riddled his interior, the depths of despair that his grin presumably concealed. Her heart went out to everyone. She beamed at them her most supportive smile—an anguished rictus, in fact, which so monstrously contorted her face that everyone in the room generously hoped that she would be first to see a doctor.

June knew how busy and tired and overworked and footsore the doctors and nurses must be (she imagined them coming home to their small but cozy apartments after sixteen-hour shifts, shouldering the door closed with a sigh, putting on their slippers, running a bath, making a nice pot of tea), and she did not want to be a bother. So she merely gazed at them plaintively as they came and went. None of them met her eye. She tried to guess from their posture, demeanor, and pace whether they had seen a little old woman die that day, or whether on the contrary they had seen a little old woman miraculously recover. When this proved inconclusive, June began to roam the halls and peer into rooms—while making herself appear as small and healthy and self-sufficient as possible.

She saw a man in a cast and thought how nasty it would be to have a broken leg. Then she thought how terrible it would be to have cancer. Then she thought how terrible it would be to be married to someone with cancer; then how terrible to have a child with cancer; then how terrible to be the doctor of a child with cancer and be unable to help … In one of the patient's rooms she glimpsed a bouquet of flowers and her optimism rebounded. How marvelous it would be to be that doctor, and be able to cure that child's cancer! And how wonderful it would be to be that child's mother; and how wonderful to be that child! Doctors and nurses, she mused, really were heroes … Perhaps she would write a novel about a child with cancer …

She turned a corner and heard a voice she recognized scream, "*I don't want to go in there!*"

The scream was so bloodcurdling that June could only picture a gang of thugs shoving poor Mrs. Drax down a manhole or stuffing her into a body bag. June ran down the hall to the old woman's rescue.

She paused in the doorway to reevaluate the situation. Reginalda Drax sat propped up by pillows in a hospital bed, the clean white sheets pulled snugly up to her chin. Several feet away, well beyond shoving or stuffing range, stood a short, sad, serious doctor or nurse (June could not tell them apart) with one hand on a wheelchair and the other holding a clipboard.

"I'm not getting anywhere near that infernal contraption and that's that!" cried Mrs. Drax. When her mouth flew open and her voice came roaring out, her head seemed disembodied, swaddled there in the bedclothes. To June she said, "Who are you? Get out of my room. I asked for a private room, not a room filled with smelly zombies!"

The doctor or nurse turned to June. He had a wide, unhappy mouth, which he opened minimally to ask if she was the family.

Mrs. Drax was aghast. She denied that she had ever seen this strange woman before, much less been related to her.

June twisted a toe into the linoleum, glanced left and right, and coughed into her fist. It occurred to her that perhaps the sight of the person who had run her over would not be a wholly welcome one to Mrs. Drax. Modulating the truth uneasily, June said, "I was at the scene of the accident. Is she—all right?"

"There's nothing wrong with me! What're you asking him for? He's as much a quack as all the others. I had sciatica for twelve years before they diagnosed it right. Don't talk about me like I'm not in the room. I *am* in the room. This is my room! I asked for a private room!"

The nurse or doctor took June aside, and with sober candor, showed her the X-rays. The bones, he explained, showed white; the breaks in the bones were black. June gasped: Mrs. Drax's skeleton looked like something that had been uncovered by archeologists—or rather, something that had been baked in an oven, methodically shattered with a hammer, then uncovered thousands of years later by archeologists.

"Frankly," said the nurse or doctor, underscoring his frankness by gazing into June's eyes before continuing, "frankly, it's amazing she's even alive."

June winced. Mrs. Drax said that if they thought she couldn't hear what they were whispering over there they were crazy; she could hear a pin hit carpet at fifty yards; and if they thought she was going to let them stick a pink chunk of foreign plastic in her ear they had another thing coming. "I'm not getting in no wheelchair neither. There's nothing wrong with my legs. Just give me my walker and get out of my way!"

The doctor or nurse looked sadly at the old woman. "Mrs. Drax," he said, "you have been in a very serious accident."

Reginalda Drax denied that this was so.

"You've just come from four hours of intensive reconstructive surgery."

Reginalda Drax said that she had not authorized it and would not pay for it.

"The surgeons did everything in their power, but it is, frankly, unlikely, given the extent of the injuries, that you will ever be able to walk again."

Mrs. Drax said that if they would give her her walker she would walk on their graves.

"Mrs. Drax, I—Your walker, it's—" A sob of guilt escaped June. "It's completely broken!"

"There's nothing wrong with my walker that a drop of oil won't fix. People these days! A little squeak in the wheel and they throw it on the trash heap. A little wear in the soles and they're out buying a new pair of shoes. They're down there at the landfill burning up piles of tires with perfectly good treads on them as we speak. How much tread do you need on the roads around here? You'd think they were at the North Pole or someplace. Snow chains in July! I've seen it!" She peered distrustfully at June. "What're you, chunkalunk, some kind of wandering sales rep for the walker makers? Get out of my room, and take these stinky geezers with you!"

June's mouth fell moistly open. "The poor dear," she reasoned, "she must be in terrible pain."

The nurse or doctor shrugged. "She won't let us give her anything."

"When can she go home?"

"When I was a girl," Mrs. Drax was saying, "they made things to last. And we knew how to darn a sock, let me tell you. When our building was put on the boiler my mother'd save the lukewarm water that came out before it ran hot. We knew how to stretch a penny, by God! Not like this bunch of charlatans! You know how much they charged my George for a sprained finger—his *little* finger?"

"Frankly," said the doctor or nurse, "the sooner the better."

AT EIGHT, REGINALDA DISCOVERED BOOKS. At twelve, she discovered boys. Boys seemed not to like smart girls, so she resolved to give up books and to expunge from her vocabulary all incriminatingly clever words—starting with "expunge" and "incriminatingly." After several unsatisfactory dalliances, she decided instead, at age fourteen, to give up boys. From then on, whenever she was introduced to a boy, she hit at him with large words and literary non sequiturs until he went away. Over time this policy became, as all our policies become, a stereotyped habit. Borrowing a sentence from the heroine of one of her favorite books, she took to saying, on meeting anyone new, "What is your name, and how did you come here, and what are these wet things in this great bag?" It became part of her idiolect. No one understood what it meant; she forgot its origin herself. Then one day, when she was eighteen, a young man quoted back to her the subsequent line: "You had better let them alone; they are loaches for my mother." It was as if a key had turned deep inside her. They married, and lived happily and unhappily together for thirty years. When George died suddenly, the key turned back and fell out of the lock. She expected daily to die from grief—an expectation that eventually outlived her grief. Twenty years of tomorrows had been unable to shake the conviction that she was going to die soon—tomorrow, probably. Meanwhile the anger she had felt at George's dying lost precision and became anger at him. She came to believe that she had married badly, that he had been cruel to her, that they had never been happy. She'd made a mistake: she'd been tricked by a silly coincidence and a half-submerged memory. A children's book had made a fool of her. Never again. From now on she would assume that others were selfish and cruel and would hurt her if given the chance. She would not give them the chance; she would not give them an opening. And so at seventy she went through the world as if with eyes closed, that no one might poke them.

REGINALDA WAS ON HER WAY to see her sons. She went to see them every day, as she did everything she did every day— because she was not long for this world.

She was not afraid of death; in fact she found it useful. Because her time was so limited, she was obliged to avoid irritants and bores, and other people were obliged to treat her kindly, or indulgently. Her sons, who treated her neither kindly nor indulgently, had at least to make time for her every day if they did not want to find themselves left out of her will. They protested that they didn't care a damn about any will, but she knew better. After all, they made time for her every day.

Reginalda waited to cross the street to the taxi stand. It was a busy street; she had been waiting a long time. As soon as she saw an opening (that is, as soon as the street was quite empty), another car would burst onto the scene—several blocks away perhaps, but bearing down fast. People nowadays never stopped for pedestrians; in fact, they sped up when they saw you, either to beat you to the crosswalk or to frighten you back to the sidewalk. She considered the satisfaction that throwing herself under one of these hot rods would give her, and the lesson it would teach these drivers. But this was a daydream: she was no longer capable of throwing herself under anything, or anywhere. She wasn't as spry as she'd once been. Indeed, Reginalda shuffled along behind her walker so slowly that onlookers were overwhelmed by what they took to be this little old lady's superhuman tenacity. In fact, she just moved slow.

She was moving in this way when the accident happened. Suddenly she found herself lying in the street. This sort of thing was occurring more often lately. She blamed it on bad pavement. No one walked anymore these days, so no one cared if the sidewalks were a deadly obstacle course. Possibly someone had knocked her down—she remembered being jostled. She didn't need anyone to help her up; she just needed someone to put her walker in arm's reach. But no one wanted to get involved nowadays. They were all scared of lawsuits. They'd sooner watch you drown than toss you a lifesaver they weren't accredited and authorized to toss. Passersby passed by, bystanders stood by, people stepped over and around her until finally a doctor was dragged in. But doctors were no better than mechanics: if they got their claws into you, they didn't let go till they'd extracted something expensive. Suddenly she found herself in a hospital. All this fuss over a little spill!

She enjoyed the wheelchair more than she thought she would. Obviously the doctors were in cahoots with the wheelchair crowd, but Reginalda hadn't signed anything and she figured she might as well make the saleslady earn her commission. So they went for a little test drive. It was almost as comfortable as her rocking chair at home, but had the great advantage over that seat of being completely and effortlessly mobile. All she had to do was screech "Left!" or "Right!" or "Straight!" or "Step on it!" or "Slow down!" or "Hold on!" and the wheelchair instantly complied. (And because it complied instantly Reginalda took care to screech her commands at the last possible moment.) She took a ride around the park, up and down the lanes of the shopping district, and even in and out of an elevator in the courthouse downtown, just to prove that it could be done. People got out of your way when you were in a moving vehicle, by God! Then she remembered that she had been going to see her sons. To test the chair's batteries, as it were, she pointed the saleslady east on Harper Street, told her to keep an eye peeled for Garland Road (several miles distant), and took a little nap.

JUNE COULD ENDURE SUCH TREATMENT for just as long as she still believed that Mrs. Drax was suffering. But when Bobby Drax assured her that his mother was always cranky like this (he used a different word, but June preferred "cranky"), her sympathy for the old woman evaporated. She gave Bobby Drax her phone number, address, and email, and then—

"Hey, where you going, chubalub?"

—June went home.

That night, however, she couldn't sleep. Her dogs sensed it, and couldn't sleep either. So she put a pot of milk on the stove and they all sat up, thinking. She could not guess what weighed on their little minds; but occasionally, when her own thoughts bubbled over into speech—"That terrible woman!"—the dogs lifted their ears and gazed at her quizzically and compassionately. Then she felt obliged to explain herself and minimize her outburst in a reassuring tone. But as the night wore on, her outbursts became more frequent and her tone less and less reassuring.

Her first instinct was to turn Mrs. Drax into fiction, to make her a character in a novel. For June's defense against anything unpleasant was that of the holiday traveller's: "Oh well—it'll make a good story when we get home!" (It is this belief, that all nastiness can be transmuted usefully into anecdote or art, that misleads some writers to the converse belief: that all art has its origins in nastiness—that we learn in suffering what we teach in song. This is flattering to the artist, for everyone likes to think he has suffered more than most. But June, who suffered little, did not fall prey to this fallacy. She knew that she wrote best when she was most cheerful.)

The problem was that Mrs. Drax would not make a good character. She was too unlikeable, too unsympathetic, to be believed. June's readers would object that no one so selfish, so cranky, so rude had ever existed or could ever exist. And June felt that they would be right. And yet, nevertheless, the woman did exist. It was a problem.

Perhaps there were some things—some people—who simply did not belong in fiction. But this contradicted June's faith in the comprehensive inclusiveness of fiction, and of her own fiction in particular. Though she was too modest to put it into words, she felt that one of her great qualities as a novelist was that she featured every kind of person in her novels—or would eventually, or could. As it happened, she did not have to put this thought into words: someone had done it for her. On every edition of every book that she had published since 1990 there appeared the testimony of *The Philadelphia Enquirer* that June Cottan had a "keenly wide-ranging sympathy." She did not understand exactly how width of range could be keen, but never mind—the point was that her sympathy was wide-ranging. But now, for the first time, she had begun to doubt her own blurbs. It was a dark night of the soul indeed.

She was brutal with herself: Had she *ever* written an unsympathetic character? It seemed to her that she had not. When her characters acted meanly or cruelly they always had a good reason or a good excuse. When they suffered they suffered only from misunderstandings or momentary weaknesses, never from malice or hatred. Where, in all her works, was Evil? For surely Evil existed in the world. How else did one explain war? How did one account for the Holocaust? But then where was June Cottan's war novel, her Holocaust novel? For a time (because it is easier to write ten books than to change the way we act towards even one little old lady) June lost herself in daydreams of the Holocaust novel she would write. In her vision, all the Nazis had different faces, but they all sneered and screeched like Mrs. Drax.

At last she recollected herself. She was already working on a novel; where were the villains in *it*? Leora's parents were not villains, though they forced her to marry rich, old, ugly Mr. Man der Lynn. Poor themselves, they wanted to save their only daughter from poverty; having married for love themselves, they wanted to save her from the disappointments that drudgery and routine bring, as they believed, to all lovers. But they meant well. And Mr. Man der Lynn was not a villain, though he forbade her to see her beloved Alex. He was merely old-fashioned and terrified of scandal; he tried but failed to share her youthful enthusiasms—but he *tried*; and in the end, when he was made to see her true heart's desires, he dissolved their marriage readily enough. For he too meant well, and wanted only to do what was right.

Why? Why did all her characters mean well and do right? Why did none of them mean ill or do wrong? Why, oh why, were all her characters so damn spineless?

Because they were sympathetic. But what did that mean? It meant that they were someone you could sympathize with. But shouldn't a nice person be able to sympathize with anyone, no matter how nasty? Wasn't that the whole *point* of literature—that it gave you, the reader, practice in feeling sympathy for people who were different from you? Practice in adopting other people's points of view?

But if that were so—and June had never questioned it— then it was almost a moral imperative to make one's characters as different, as alien, as *un*sympathetic as possible. Otherwise the reader had no gap to cross. June's characters, it now seemed to her, were wickedly easy to sympathize with; nothing whatsoever prevented the reader from identifying with them. They were generic and inoffensive. They were normal; they were bland. They liked nice things and disliked nasty things. They had only mild quirks and were driven by only the most common motives and desires. They were in fact hollow shells—mere costumes that the reader could comfortably wear, masks through which the reader could comfortably peer. That was what sympathizing with, identifying with, or rooting for a character really was: *becoming* them! Or rather, making them become you. It was not a way of getting inside another person's head; it was a way of getting your own head inside another body, and, through that body, of experiencing another world, living another life. Perhaps, after all, literature was not bettering or broadening, but just another means of escape. Perhaps fiction in fact only gave you practice at being yourself in exotic situations. Perhaps, by inviting you to cheer for the good guys and despise the bad guys, fiction only taught you how to better cheer for yourself and despise everyone else. By reinforcing the niceness of nice things and the nastiness of nasty things, perhaps fiction only entrenched you more firmly and inescapably in your own limited self. Perhaps novels were, after all, immoral.

For a long time June stood rigidly over the stove, stirring and staring into the pot of milk as though trying to make it boil by willpower alone.

She saw in her mind the startled, shriveled face, and heard again the terrible thud.

"No!" she cried, and threw down the spoon; the dogs started. "Fiction is not immoral," she muttered. "*I* am."

And she resolved to revisit Mrs. Drax—poor, lonely, hurting Mrs. Drax—just as soon as she'd finished the chapter she was working on.

THEY SOON DEVELOPED A ROUTINE. June was permitted to write for two hours in the morning, then she would report to the nursing home to take Mrs. Drax on her daily rounds. Their first stop was the Salvation Army, where Mrs. Drax bought up all the second-hand sweaters, which she unraveled and made into sweaters; she believed this was cheaper than buying yarn. (It was not.) Then they visited the library, where Mrs. Drax traded one Shakespeare for another hopefully less boring one. (She would not let June read to her from anything but Shakespeare, because Shakespeare was the best there was, and he was bad enough.) Next was the bulk department of the grocery store, where Mrs. Drax bought her day's supply of caraway seeds, which she liked to chew when she was not doing anything else with her mouth. (Fifteen seeds cost her $0.03.) Then came lunch, or rather the argument over where to go for lunch. Mrs. Drax's method was to insist that she did not care where they went, then to find fault with every one of June's suggestions until she hit upon the place that Mrs. Drax had had in mind all along. The afternoon was dedicated to Mrs. Drax's solicitor, whose job it was to amend her will and to subtract from her estate the cost of his services. Surprisingly, Mrs. Drax's will was only symbolically vindictive. If one of her sons had treated her badly the day before, she lowered his share of the inheritance to forty-eight percent and boosted the other's to fifty-two; if they had both treated her badly, they split it down the middle. She occasionally lamented that she could not give the whole amount away to a charity or church; but charities nowadays were nothing but a tax dodge for sleazy corporations, and religion was for dopes. Sometimes she looked pointedly at June and asked the lawyer leading questions which revealed that no one but her sons would ever get any of her money. The bulk of her amendments were not legally significant, but more in the nature of appeals or advice to the living. She asked the management of Green Oaks to commemorate her by removing the meat loaf from their menu; she urged Mrs. McGillicuddy to finish the blue sweater she was knitting, but, NB, to use a garter stitch where the pattern recommended a stockinette; she didn't care who did it, but would someone please check her Sunday crossword answers—she wasn't too sure about 32 Down being "shotput." After the solicitor came visits to Mrs. Drax's sons, one of whom usually gave them supper, if Mrs. Drax denied stridently enough that they were hungry. Then Mrs. Drax was taken to the first thirty minutes of some movie, which, as she explained loudly and patiently to the audience at large, was about all she could handle, movies these days being too fast, too silly, too violent, or too raunchy for her taste. Then June rolled her back to the nursing home for bridge, knitting, Shakespeare, and, ostensibly, death. It was usually ten o'clock by the time June got home to her poor neglected dogs, who had not been out for a walk since dawn.

This regimen was hard on the dogs; but it was hard on June too. For one thing, she was not used to walking twenty-odd miles a day. (Mrs. Drax could not explain why the sight of June's crumpled car filled her with revulsion and panic, and June did not press her.) She could not take the dogs along, either, because Mrs. Drax did not like dogs, and dogs did not like her. When she and June's dogs were in the same room together the dogs stood on one side and barked at Mrs. Drax while she sat on the other side and yelled right back at them, as though they were all debating some controversial new traffic law in town hall. And though June normally liked walking, since it gave her the opportunity to wave at her neighbors and smile kindly at strangers, she found that no one smiled back when she was with Mrs. Drax, who scowled at everyone: postmen, children, and panhandlers—especially panhandlers, whom she called "dirty bums" or "lazy beggars," advised to seek employment, and sometimes spat at. June, who was flustered by panhandlers (she found that they made her feel awkward, privileged, and ungenerous whether she gave them spare change or not), was positively mortified by Mrs. Drax's behavior. She apologized profusely and gave them all ten-dollar bills—so that, in time, the bums on their downtown route came to relish

Mrs. Drax's maltreatment, and even to like her a little; while June, they felt, was a "dumb cluck" and a "three-minute egg."

Life with Mrs. Drax was not always so terrible. One day, while they rolled down Harper Street, Mrs. Drax napped in her chair, her head lolling back, and the sight of her puckered face, petulant even in sleep, gave June sentimental daydreams about a daughter who moves back home to nurse her dying mother...

June no longer wondered why Mrs. Drax was such a nasty person. When Mrs. Drax was awake, the question did not grip the imagination. When Mrs. Drax went rigid with frustration at some perceived wrong, thrusting out her pelvis and kicking her legs, or crumpled into a seething, trembling bomb of resentment, or exploded in a fulminating tantrum, it didn't seem to matter much whether she acted this way because she had been spoiled as a child or deprived as an adolescent, or because her parents had been disgracefully poor or disgracefully rich, or because she had been forced to marry a man she did not love or had lost the one she did. Anything was possible; and probably at least one explanation was correct. But because Mrs. Drax was not a character in a novel, June could never know the real reasons. The thing to remember, she felt, was that there *was* some explanation. Nasty people were not born nasty, and did not choose to be nasty just for the fun of it. Something turned them that way; it was not their fault—so one could have sympathy for them. Or so at least June felt while Mrs. Drax slept.

When Reginalda awoke, she caught June looking at her tenderly.

She understood by this time that June was no saleslady for a wheelchair manufacturer, but rather some kind of novelist—in other words, a filthy liar. The woman was obviously a con artist; why else would she be nice? Besides, no one cheerful could be for real. She was so cheerful she was skittish. She spoke in a chipper telemarketer's voice, as if afraid you'd hang up on her before she could get her hooks in. And Reginalda did not like the way she peered out at you over her fat cheeks, like some cagey woodland rodent peering out of a hollow tree. The kinder and more considerate June was, the more Reginalda distrusted and disliked her.

"What are *you* looking at? Eyes on the road, short stack! You trying to break my legs on a telephone pole?"

June's sympathetic daydreams fled; she bit her lip and sighed; her exasperation overflowed into speech before she could catch herself. "We're not even moving, Reginalda. It's a stop light."

Reginalda believed that only weak, fickle people corrected themselves. "I know what a stop light is!" she screeched. Bystanders turned to look censoriously at June. What was she doing to that poor old lady?

The light changed, but June did not move.

"What's the hold up? Get a move on, slowpoke!"

June gazed sadly into Mrs. Drax's face. She tried to explain how unnecessary all this nastiness was. "Don't you— It isn't— We don't have to—" She gasped in frustration. If only she could write Mrs. Drax a nice long letter! "Darnit, Reginalda, I'm on your side. You don't have to be so,"—she shook her arms and stamped her feet to illustrate Mrs. Drax's character—"all the time, anymore. You know? Okay?"

A breathless gust of fear passed through Reginalda. She confused it for anger; then it became anger. She could no more identify the cause of this anger than she could have identified the genus of tree burning in a fireplace. Nor was she inclined to introspection. All she knew was that this tubby, meddlesome sneak was lecturing her. She lost her temper.

She swore and snorted and spat and flailed till the unmended bones in her arms and legs broke again. She bucked the wheelchair into the street and it began to roll downhill. June screamed and ran after it.

Late that night, after many hours at the hospital, June brought Mrs. Drax home. She put her in her own bedroom and made her as comfortable as possible in her new wheelchair; Mrs. Drax told her to keep her dirty sausage fingers to herself and to mind her own business. Then June went upstairs and locked herself in the attic, so that the dogs would not hear her cry.

PADDY GERCHESZKY

THE ELEVATOR DOORS closed, and Gercheszky began to sweat. He was not claustrophobic; he was alone. There was no one in the elevator for him to talk to. He needed to talk like a shark needs to swim. His thoughts, given no outlet, grew toxic and turbulent, like thoughts in a fever dream.

He was on his way to a party, and though he loved parties he worried that this party would be a bad one. He would know no one; worse, no one would know him. No women would be there; worse, no one famous. He would say something foolish and everyone would laugh at him; worse, no one would laugh, no one would pay any attention to him, no one would notice him at all.

Fretfully he began rehearsing the funny and interesting things he would say—he had a fund of these. What he really needed was a good entrance, something that would draw all eyes to him from the first moment he stepped through the door. He had a fund of these too. Should he do the blind-man shtick? The porno plumber bit? The missing penguin gag? By the time he emerged from the elevator he was drenched.

He found the apartment, dropped his trousers, and threw open the door like a man entering his own bathroom—an impersonation he had intended to garnish with the cry, "What are all you people doing in my bathroom?" But he did not get the words out, for there was no one there to hear them.

It was his worst fear: He was too late. The party was over. Great things had been said and done by beautiful and powerful people and Paddy Gercheszky had not been among them.

A woman in a bathrobe appeared, drying a plate. "You're bleeding," she said.

The sweat had caused a razor cut on his cheek to reopen. He stared at her with wild incomprehension, his pants around his ankles.

In fact, as usual, Gercheszky was early.

GERCHESZKY WAS A TALKER, not a writer. His handwriting was atrocious and his spelling notorious. He loved words, but he knew them by sound, not by sight. One time, going over the galleys of a novel, he had crossed out every instance of a strange new word, one which appeared to him to be the sound that a spring makes when it is plucked. He had never encountered the word "doing" in print before.

His ignorance was ostensibly explained by his claim that, till the time he immigrated to New York at age twenty, he had spoken only Yiddish and French. Amazingly, Gercheszky spoke impeccable English with only the faintest Canadian accent. Nor had any living soul ever heard him speak a word of French or Yiddish—though certainly he was known to season his talk with exotic idioms, implied to be Québécois, and occasionally his speech took on Yiddish cadences. If he refused to speak his mother tongues, it was, he said, because they brought back sad memories, and because now he was in America, and "in Rome one must as the Romans do."

He sometimes lapsed like this into infelicity, as if suddenly remembering his role as foreigner. But he also knew that his solecisms gave good entertainment value. He had heard the story about the multi-million-dollar computer that had translated the phrase "The spirit is willing, but the flesh is weak" into Russian as "The vodka is okay, but the meat is rotten." He adopted this as one of his catchphrases, and invented others. "If beggars had pigs, then wishes would fly." "You can kick a dead horse in the mouth but you can't make him drink."

He was perhaps less successful when, in telling a joke, he feigned ignorance of double entendres. For example: What is the difference between outlaws and in-laws? The correct punchline is "Outlaws are wanted." But Gercheszky put the case more bluntly: "Nobody likes in-laws! Ha ha ha!"

LATER, AT A BETTER PARTY, Gercheszky bustled from group to group, making clever comments over people's shoulders. To a senator's aide and the sister of a film director who were both wearing grey he said, "Look at you two! Did you call each other up before the party and coordinate?" They smiled but gave him no opening into their conversation—some crap about *The Catcher in the Rye* or some other piece of crap he had never read. Gercheszky, the novelist, hated books.

Eventually he gave up and hovered near the snack table. When at last a couple took the bait, Gercheszky pounced. "You're wondering about my hat," he told them. They were too polite to deny it; besides, their mouths were full. Gercheszky did not share such qualms: through a mouthful of shrimp cocktail, he told them about his childhood.

At first, as he spoke, they watched rather than listened to him. Gercheszky was wonderful to watch. First you noticed the funny hat, the hairy knuckles, the flaring nostrils, and the shrimp juice dribbling down the chin. Then all those petty details were whipped into a blur of insignificance by the whirlwind spectacle of his vivacity. His energy was astounding; his exuberance made blasé people feel envious and guilty. When he told a story, his entire body was enlisted: his hands conjured shapes and relations; his chest inflated or collapsed to illustrate a character's stature; his eyes danced, and shone on each of his listeners in turn, so that even in a crowd you felt like Gercheszky was speaking to you alone. And then there was his face. One moment it was furrowed with anguish, the next twisted in befuddlement; now taut with rage, now drooping in melancholy, now slack with awe and relief.

Meanwhile his voice boomed and whispered and tinkled and guffawed. People started to hear what he was saying; his spectators became an audience. As the buttonholed couple listened to his tale, their faces lost their wariness, and gradually became blank with rapture. Others who came for the hors d'oeuvres were drawn in by the story. Before long Gercheszky was addressing every person at the party, the senator's aide and director's sister included. They all stood clustered around him, jostling for the best positions like a crowd at a crime scene, close enough that his gestures sometimes knocked the drinks out of their hands. They didn't even notice. Words of wonder and indignation fell from their loose, pendulous lips.

"… Boiled bread!?"

"… Fifteen cents!?"

"… Only four years old!?"

"… An igloo!?"

"… With both fists!?"

"… And still you ate it!?"

"… The police too!?"

"… Right out into the street!?"

"… Not a word of English!?"

"… And her a nun!?"

He never did get around to an explanation of his hat—an oily, balding patchwork of squirrel skins—because, for every newcomer, he started his story again from the beginning. And with each retelling, the story became only more amazing, saddening, and inspiring.

Years later, at other parties, people who were tired of Paddy Gercheszky would point to these embellishments as proof that he had made it all up. In fact, Gercheszky always held back details for later iterations, so that those who had come early would not be bored. He was a consummate storyteller.

And he had made it all up.

GERCHESZKY DICTATED HIS NOVELS, of course. His friends took turns as secretary, or pooled their resources to hire one. The professionals rarely stuck around for more than one draft. Revision to Gercheszky meant telling the same story again, but better. To his secretaries it meant needlessly transcribing the same story again in different words. This practice won Gercheszky a reputation for perfectionism among people who did not work with him.

Years later, his wife bought him a tape recorder. Gercheszky would come home after a party and fill three or four spools, till he was exhausted enough to sleep for an hour or two. Unlike Dickens, who imagined his characters milling about his desk as he wrote, Gercheszky imagined his audience. He imagined himself, in fact, at a party—always a slightly better party than the one he had just left. As the tapes attest, he often addressed his phantom auditors by name, paused for their replies and questions, and laughed with avuncular affection at their naivety and delight. And though Gercheszky's transcribers and editors excluded from their texts this apostrophizing, the novels retain an intimate and hortatory quality. Every paragraph seems prefaced with an urgent "Now listen—"

LATER, AT A BETTER PARTY, he watched a woman patiently smooth her long brown hair into separate strands with her thumbnail. He approached her and said, "Haven't I seen you on television?"

"I don't think so."

"Oh," he laughed, "I must have been thinking of me."

Her companion said, "You've been on television?"

"Oh sure." Gercheszky told them about his appearances on Hal Patly, the Ed Sullivan of the Bronx. The couple stared blankly. He produced a copy of his own novel (he had planted it on the bookshelf earlier that evening), but the couple could not be made to recognize his name. His attention began to wander. Even as he told them the horrible, uplifting tale of his childhood in the Jewish quarter of Old Montreal, his gaze drifted towards the door. When a semi-famous actress came in, he excused himself.

"Hey," he said, meaning: I know your face but I can't remember your name.

"Hey," she said, which he took to mean: Thank you.

"Remember me?" he said, meaning: Recognize me?

"I *think* so ..."

He took this to mean: Yes. His posture relaxed; though, as always—even when talking to someone famous, even when seated next to Hal Patly on Channel 16—one of his shoulders remained thrust forward, as if he had been caught mid-stride. He always looked like he was on his way somewhere. He was.

He looked the actress over approvingly, like an old friend, and said the first thing that came into his head. (Once, at a funeral and hungry, he'd asked the mourners in the next pew if they had any food.) "I don't mean to be rude here, but are you pregnant or just putting on some flab?"

Several people in earshot showed that they were shocked. The actress, who had not even informed her lover yet, was, however, a professional. She laughed easily and took Paddy by the arm and gave him a piece of friendly advice: "Don't ever ask a woman that." Even as she feigned nonchalance, she felt the shock and fear draining away. Besides, it was simply too ridiculous to be offended by this clumsy bear of a man who wore some kind of beaver pelt on his head and blurted questions like a child. She began to feel protective of him, almost motherly, and listened indulgently as he told her the horrible, uplifting tale of his childhood in the Jewish quarter of Old Montreal.

Later, she took him to a better party. When she allowed him to give her his number, inscribed in a copy of his novel, he swore that he would not leave the apartment till she called. She believed him—he believed himself at that moment— and, feeling sorry for him, called the next day. He wasn't home. Gercheszky never went home if he could help it.

She saw him eventually at another party. Later, at yet another party, they got married.

GERCHESZKY WAS NOT A GREAT WIT. He was funny, and clever, and incisive, as his novels show, but his mind was not swift. He suffered constantly from *l'esprit de l'escalier*. Brilliant retorts occurred to him minutes and sometimes hours too late. So, rather than risk seeming oafish, Gercheszky came prepared—with anecdotes, jokes, gags, bits, and market-tested witticisms to suit any occasion.

But there are other dangers than being slow; one can also be too quick. This pitfall might be called *l'esprit de la sonnette*: Instead of coming to you too late, your witticism comes to you too early—not on your way down the stairs, but while you're still ringing the doorbell. When one comes prepared, one runs the risk of seeming glib or rehearsed.

Gercheszky was too skilled and flamboyant a speaker for that; he told even his oldest stories as if they had just happened to him minutes ago. But there is another drawback to always knowing in advance exactly what you are going to say. Gercheszky, over time, began to bore himself.

LATER, AT ANOTHER PARTY, Gercheszky told the story of how he had written his first novel—a story which most of his friends had heard before, or read about in his second novel, or both. Sensing that he was losing their attention, he segued into the story of how his second novel had come to be written. Still he sensed some fidgeting at the back of the room, so he decided to ham things up a bit. He answered the phone as if it had rung and carried on a dramatic dialogue with the imaginary caller, whose side of the conversation he revealed by asking long expository questions like a character in a bad play: "And that's when Mildred collided with a tree and broke her leg, and you had to ski down to the lodge to call an ambulance which they had to send up the mountain on a giant toboggan? Boy!" Then he went around the room picking up disgusting or inedible things which he persuaded people to dare him to eat. Swallowing a D-cell battery turned out to be something of a showstopper, so he moved on to constructing Drano bombs, shaking them and throwing them off the balcony and into the street. This livened things up until a little old lady in a wheelchair was allegedly blinded, at which point everyone became sanctimonious and pretended to lose interest in the game.

"Hey, Guggenheim! Where do you think *you're* going?"

"Aw, come on, Paddy, I've got to work in the morning."

So Gercheszky told his friends to go fuck themselves, and went to a different party—where he was upstaged by a seven-year-old ballerina.

"And this we pay money to see?" he grumbled. "She hasn't even got coordination. Heck, *I* can dance better than that." He showed them. "There!" he gasped. "And not one lesson have I had!" But it was obvious that his friends stubbornly preferred the child's clumsy kitsch to Gercheszky's intuitive artistry. The ballerina, he later discovered, was the host's daughter—which explained everything. "As an orphan," he quipped, "I hate nepotism." He wandered around the apartment criticizing the expensive furnishings. For old times' sake, he secreted under his hat a crystal vase which he thought he could probably hock, though he didn't exactly need the money these days. Finally with a honking sigh he went to sulk in the kitchen.

"I hate kids," he told a famous actress who was snorting coke and whom he was pretty sure he'd slept with once.

"Aw," she sniffed philosophically, "it's different when they're your own, Paddy."

"Yeah," he said, "when they're yours you can smack 'em."

He was so pleased with this witticism that he had to hurry to another party to repeat it. But somehow it wasn't as funny the second time, or the third, or the fourth...

GERCHESZKY NEVER CALLED HIMSELF a novelist. He found the term pigeonholing. He thought of himself as someone who, among other things, wrote novels. He had made it big because of the novels, perhaps, but he could just as easily have made it big in another field—and still might.

He often considered entering politics. He could see himself as the mayor of someplace, or the President of the United

States, or something like that. At other times, he fancied himself an entrepreneur. He believed that fortunes were built on ideas. With a good idea, any bozo could make a million, while not even a genius or superman could wring a profit from a bad one. And Gercheszky was overflowing with ideas. They came to him everywhere. One night at a party, for instance, he stood on the patio for hours, watching people through the glass doors and occasionally knocking and beckoning. He laughed every time another stranger wandered over with the same look of prospective recognition on their face. What started as a joke developed into a business plan by way of a generalization: "People love looking at other people through windows." He would open the first human zoo! Visitors on one side of the glass would pay to stare and point at visitors on the other. "The beauty part? No overhead!" Generally, however, Gercheszky found his inspiration in words. The next best thing to a good product idea was a good name. A good name usually involved a good pun. He would open a chain of coffee shops called Bean and Nothingness, or an eyeglass store called I Wear Eyewear, or a Canadian-themed credit union called MountieBank. (Gercheszky knew what a mountebank was, but assumed his clients would not—that was the beauty part.)

Another way he might distinguish himself was through investments—that is, by buying things. Gercheszky considered himself a canny investor. When he had money, he spent it fiercely, as if the stuff scalded him. He saw expense as proof of value and a guarantee of good return on investment. The more overpriced an object the better; he often haggled *up*. Some of his friends saw in this allergy to money the absent-minded unworldliness of the artist. Others, less charitable, called it stupidity. Still others believed Gercheszky desperate to acquire the symbols of status and success.

The truth, I believe, lies elsewhere. Gercheszky often called himself lazy—an adjective that no one who had seen him would ever think to apply to a man so obviously brimming over with schemes, ambitions, and energy, and that no one who had read him would ever use to describe an author in whose torrential prose even the punctuation marks are washed clean away. Nor was Gercheszky prone to false modesty; his was genuine enough. He may occasionally have painted himself in his stories as more down and out than he actually had been, but this was for dramatic interest. The flaws, obsessions, and weaknesses that he gave his narrators really were his own. Assuming, then, that Gercheszky believed himself to be lazy, it makes sense that he would go to such lengths to stay broke. Poverty forced him to keep busy. Desperation lit a fire under him. He wanted to be rich and famous, but he dreaded the indolence that riches would allow.

LATER, AT YET ANOTHER PARTY, some girl was talking to him. His attention wandered violently, shooting out in all directions like a frightened hunter lost in the woods. Everyone who came in the door was famous, beautiful, and powerful, but to Gercheszky they seemed ugly and dull because they had all heard his stories already, and had even told him some of theirs.

"…put people on diets," the girl was saying.

"Yeah? Maybe you could put *me* on a diet. People say I eat too many batteries."

When he had explained this joke, the girl said, "No no no, I'm a *dietician*. I don't *put people* on diets. That's what people *think* I do."

"Uh-huh." Why was he talking to her? Because from behind she had looked beautiful but her face was plain, and he had been puzzled and intrigued by the contradiction. And because he had never seen her around at any parties, and had assumed therefore that she hadn't heard his stories. But it turned out that she'd read them. Why had he ever written those novels? Why had he let those publishing sons of bitches bleed him dry?

Some thumping came from the ceiling and the girl said it sounded like they were having more fun upstairs.

"Don't count on it," said Gercheszky. "It's the same all over. You just can't hear the parties happening downstairs."

The girl assumed he was drunk. He wasn't like this on TV. On TV they could hardly get him to sit still long enough to answer a question. It was strange, standing so close to someone she had seen so many times on TV. Even though she had only a small television set, she'd assumed he would be much taller. She felt an overwhelming urge to grab him by the ears and pull him close to see if he was real.

Gercheszky was not drunk. In fact, he had never had a drink in his life. His father had been an alcoholic; but that fact—never spoken, never written down—he had forgotten long ago. He'd never had a drink because he'd never needed one.

"Oh Christ," he said. "My ex."

His ex-wife said to the girl that she could see that Paddy, as usual, wasn't letting anyone else get a word in edgewise. She was bitter because she had loved him once, worshipped him even, before realizing that while he gave a very convincing impression of being fascinated by her, he had never in fact heard a single word that had come out of her mouth. It was as if she'd married a carnival, or fallen in love with a movie—something thrilling and larger than life that could not, by its very nature, take any notice of her. It was the loneliest experience of her life.

Gercheszky told the girl a little about the marriage and the divorce.

"Oh!" The girl clapped her hands. "You're 'Eva'!"

Gercheszky's ex-wife told the girl that certain facts had been distorted in the novel, and cited several instances. Gercheszky explained to the girl the concept of artistic license. His ex-wife explained to the girl the concept of eating shit and dying.

They had a beautiful argument, which everyone gathered round to watch.

LATER, AT ANOTHER STUPID PARTY, Gercheszky read aloud passages from his fourth novel, breaking in periodically to explain how today he would write it differently. His haggard audience (the host and the hostess—everyone else had gone home hours ago) listened obediently, with the respect they believed due a great novelist, till long after the sun came up and Gercheszky's voice grew hoarse. When he caught them nodding off, he tore the book in half and threw the halves at their heads. "Go!" he screamed. "Sleep! Who's stopping you?" He stormed out of the apartment, then immediately returned, contrite. "I'll stay on the couch. Not even a peep will I make. I'll cook us all breakfast, the real traditional Jewish breakfast of Old Montreal."

Everybody knew by this time that Paddy Gercheszky was neither Jewish nor Québécois; that he had grown up in a suburb of Toronto; that he was not an orphan; that he was not even Paddy Gercheszky—his real name was Patrick Gurchase. But they all pretended not to know, because they liked Paddy, more or less, and anyway had known him longer than they had known his biographer (whom they no longer invited to their parties). Also, perhaps, they did not want to admit that they had been fooled. They chose to believe that they had always known there was something fishy about Paddy's stories, and that it hadn't mattered because he'd told them so well. As they say in Yiddish: You don't ask questions of a story.

But now his friends just wanted some sleep. "Aw, come on, Paddy. Don't be like that. There'll be other parties."

Long ago, at a better party, someone else had said words like these to him.

He'd been the life of that party: telling jokes, singing and dancing, trading insults with his uncles, entertaining everyone—his parents, his eight older siblings, and all their friends. And then they'd sent him to bed.

Alone in his room while the fun went on without him, he felt angry at first, then frightened, then strange. He felt tingly and insubstantial—like he didn't have a body, like he didn't exist.

Later, his mother sat with him amidst the wreckage—apparently he'd thrown a tantrum—and ran her fingers through his hair to calm him. "Paddy, Paddy," she said, "won't you ever go to sleep? The world will still be here in the morning."

But that was what he was afraid of: that the world would always be there; there when he woke, there when he slept; that it would just go on being there, whether he was part of it or not.

RIDING DOWN ALONE IN THE ELEVATOr, Gercheszky remembered none of this. He popped a sleeping pill so that he would pass out as soon as he got home. He had no more novels to dictate.

Downstairs in the lobby, the night watchman recognized him. Snapping his fingers, he said, "Hey, aren't you—"

"No," said Gercheszky, then added benevolently, "but I get that all the time."

The night watchman was offended. He had often seen Gercheszky on TV—the TV behind this very desk. Gercheszky should have been amazed by the coincidence and flattered by the recognition. After all, how many people sat up all night watching old reruns of Hal Patly? How many people had sat up night after night listening to Paddy Gercheszky whine about his childhood, kvetch about sex, and repent his marriage? The night watchman felt that he knew Gercheszky intimately, as few did. He and Gercheszky had shared a bond.

Well, to hell with Gercheszky. The night watchman was glad he'd never bought any of his books. They probably stunk.

FEW DO READ GERCHESZKY'S BOOKS these days—unless it is to point out where they deviate from fact. The interest in Gercheszky has shifted since his death almost entirely from the work to the man himself. The biographies now outnumber the novels by a factor of four, with more on the way each year. A Hollywood film, starring funny man Kyle Lipton, is purportedly in the works.

It is hard at first to imagine that Gercheszky would mind this trend. But then one realizes that if his life or his childhood had been more interesting, he would never have needed to become a *novelist* at all. If not the savvy investor, bold entrepreneur, politician, or movie star that he sometimes dreamed of being, he would surely have become in fact what he could only pretend in this life to be: a great memoirist masquerading as a novelist to avoid lawsuits.

I think the trend towards biography is unfortunate, because Gercheszky *was* a great storyteller. He had an instinct for what to borrow and what to leave out. His books, I believe, represent the best of him. The novelist is a sort of sculptor who hews and polishes the rough block of his life down to something beautiful and elegant. The literary biographer by contrast scrutinizes the dust and rubble on the floor, and would happily obscure the sculpture in his effort to restore the rough block to its original state. But I suppose that in writing this character sketch I am guilty of the same desecration.

The biographer of another novelist once said that poetry always triumphs over history—by which he meant that a lie well told always outlives the truth. Although parts of his legend survive—this story is called "Paddy Gercheszky" and not "Patrick Gurchase"—I am afraid that, for once, history will triumph over poetry.

THE DOOR IN THE WALL

"**HERE, DUCK**. Here, ducky duck."

Laurel Peggery sat on the edge of a park bench, scattering hunks of bread in an appetizing arrangement across the gravel bank. The duck, however, was grooming himself and took no notice.

She was a tall, sturdy, stolid woman, dressed neatly in several layers of grey thrift-store sweaters, jackets, and scarves. Her posture was scrupulously correct. A permanently furrowed forehead and deep character lines, running from her nose to the corners of her wide mouth, made her look formidable; but her eyes were moist and beseeching.

A man came ambling along the path towards her. She stuffed the loaf into her purse and kicked aside the crumbs on the ground. She crossed her knees and folded her hands and stared resolutely at the trees across the pond.

The man took no more notice of her than the duck had, and so was startled when, at the last moment, she fixed her gaze on him and said firmly, as if reproaching herself for some weakness, "Good morning." He was surprised to see that she was young and attractive. He was past her before he could return her greeting; and though he soon forgot all about the girl on the bench in the park, the rest of his day was haunted by a specter of disappointment and dissatisfaction with life.

Laurel watched him till he was out of sight, then shook herself and returned to her task.

"Here, ducky. Here, ducky duck duck duck."

A battered seagull flapped to earth twenty feet away and began strutting back and forth, watching her from alternate eyes. She hissed at it and threw a pebble in its direction, but her aim was poor and the gull, unruffled, continued its surveillance.

Suddenly a squirrel dashed out from under her bench, seized a hunk of bread in its mouth, and bounded away in undulating leaps. She hissed and stamped her feet after it.

"Filthy vermin." She glared pointedly at the seagull, who had taken advantage of the distraction to come a few steps closer.

The duck, meanwhile, had completed his washing-up and sat down at the edge of the pond with his back to her.

"Duckeeee," she whispered, holding out a golden, spongy crumb. The duck ruffled his feathers with luxurious contentment and settled more deeply into the bank.

Laurel held the crumb between her thumb and index finger before her eye, like a jeweler appraising a diamond, and, rocking her forearm, carefully took aim.

The first crumb landed in the pond, the second, somehow, in a shrub behind her, but the third landed an inch from the duck's head.

He looked at it. She held her breath.

He prodded it with his beak.

Then he picked it up, and with a toss of his head, flung it into the pond. Laurel, the duck, and the seagull watched as it grew sodden and sank below the surface.

"Oh, to hell with you," she said, and threw the rest of the loaf at the duck. Anger did not improve her aim. The bread rolled into a tuft of marsh grass, where it was promptly rescued by the seagull, who carried it across the pond and began tearing it apart and squawking. Soon the area was swarming with shrieking gulls.

Laurel kicked gravel at the duck, then got to her feet and strode home.

LIONEL PUGG MOVED TO THE CITY to get away from a girl who did not love him and promptly fell in love with a girl who would never love him. He did not know that at first; at first—indeed for four years—he didn't even know her name.

Angel was his waitress at the first café he visited, his first day in the city. She dressed carelessly, like someone at the beach; she wore oversize flip-flops and shuffled penitentially from table to table, her head cocked to one side as if peering around some corner. She took orders standing heavily on one foot. She had a bluff, brash manner that terrified and beguiled him. She nearly gave him a heart attack when she called him "dear."

"All right, what's it going to be, dear."

Though he was ravenous, he asked for a coffee, not wanting to put her to the trouble of fetching a menu.

"Is that it?" she asked irritably.

Lionel Pugg was a knobby, gangly, twitchy young man, with sunken eyes, a concave chest, and hunched shoulders. He had thin skin and more than the usual number of nerves, so he quivered like an overwhelmed antenna. Angel thought he looked like a creep.

"You can take up the table because it's slow today," she said, "but don't expect me to swoop down every five minutes to refill you, if that's all you're having. Somehow I don't peg you for a big tipper."

Lionel agreed, by gesture, that he was an abominable tipper.

He finished his coffee as quickly as its temperature allowed, left a five hundred percent tip, and fled without risking further talk or eye contact. From that day forward, he ate his meals at the café whenever Angel was not working, and sat there quaking with dread that she would appear before he could finish, and left shuddering with disappointment when she did not.

He wrote her a novel. It took him three years to complete. It was about a waitress, brash and beautiful but otherwise rather without qualities, who fell in love with one of her customers who had also fallen in love with her. This mutual affection was happily discovered one day (on page ten) when the customer asked the waitress to marry him, and she agreed. Several chapters were dedicated to the technicalities of the wedding and the details of their blissful cohabitation, but this only brought the book to page fifty-seven—a rather paltry offering, he felt. He had shown that these two would be happy together (which had been his secret didactic purpose), but perhaps their happiness had been too easily achieved? So he decided to have the waitress kidnapped; that got the ball rolling again. To make the kidnapping plausible, he had to supply the waitress with a garish back story, which reached as far back as her distant ancestors and as far forward as her decision to become a waitress. Then there was the question of the kidnappers' motives, inevitably informed by their own characters and back stories. Finally, out of fairness, Lionel felt obliged to provide the customer-protagonist with a history and pedigree too. By this point, the hero bore little resemblance to the author, and the heroine probably had as little in common with her original; but he reassured himself that the portraits were metaphorical and still recognizable. If he was not a burly secret agent in fact, he was, anyway, rather taciturn; and if Angel was not a dispossessed Balkan monarch in fact, she was, anyway, rather imperious.

Then came the action. His counterpart, the customer-protagonist, tracked the kidnappers first to their hideout in the Sierra Madre, then, from coded documents found there, to their headquarters in Washington, D.C., and from clues there, to their homes in Toronto, Phoenix, and Dublin, and from there to outposts in Brussels, Kuala Lumpur, and the moon. The waitress-heroine, meanwhile, was too beautiful and brash to remain idle. By the time her husband had hunted down and one by one killed off her kidnappers, she had successfully reverse-engineered their mind-control device and transmitted the blueprints to her Balkan accomplices. She had never been in any danger and was not grateful for the violent rescue. She divorced him, and on the last page threw her wedding ring at him and told him to get lost.

This was not as Lionel had planned. But it seemed the more he subjected his characters to situation and event, the more vivid they became, and the more vivid they became, the less control he exerted over them. Consequently his novels never ended the way he thought they should—that is, happily—but always with some vivid, attractive character telling the protagonist what his flaws were, throwing something at him, and stalking off the page. In this case, the ending rather undermined his secret didactic purpose; so he reassured himself that the heroine and hero were total fictions and had no relation whatsoever to the real waitress or himself, and that, at 458 typewritten pages, *Served Cold* was a respectable gift, a genuine love-novel.

He did not want to bother his beloved at work, so he carried the manuscript around with him for another year, hoping to run into her casually on the street. In fact, he saw Angel somewhere about town almost every other week, and on several occasions literally bumped into her. Finally, on one of these occasions she took him by the shoulders, held him upright to scrutinize his face, and demanded to know where she knew him from.

The memory of the pressure of her hands on his arms rendered him aphasic.

"I know I've seen you somewheres. Was it Lulu's? Do you know the Donkey? It wasn't the *restaurant*? Ah well: mysteries. What's that you got there? It looks big enough to be a *book*." She laughed at the outlandishness of her imagination. "Hey, I've got a date but come buy me a drink anyway in case I'm stood up. It's just across the street."

The mention of the date restored him to speech. "I couldn't possibly intrude," he said, and ran away.

At their next encounter, he did better: he thrust the manuscript into her hands, said, "I wrote this for you," and then ran away.

He stayed away from the café for six weeks. When at last he mustered the courage to return, Angel showed no sign of recognizing him. She did, however, come around with the coffee pot and refill his cup several times. Finally she asked him what he was doing that night. "I'm thinking of going to a party and I might need a date, in case it stinks."

Angel had not read the novel, but she had removed its elastic bands and identified it as a novel. She had no way of judging its worth—nor any inclination to, since it flattered her to suppose it a work of genius. Though she still thought Lionel was a creep, she began taking him around with her to parties and bars and introducing him to other more attractive men as her genius admirer. She found him useful, for she did not like to be alone.

THE MAIL HAD ARRIVED. Laurel tore open the mailbox, clutched the three letters to her chest without looking at them, hurried upstairs to her apartment, locked and bolted the door behind her, then sat down at her desk to inspect her booty.

All three envelopes were identical: the same size, the same color, with the same stamp in the same place, and all three addressed in the same meticulous handwriting—her handwriting. Three more of her self-addressed stamped envelopes had found their way back to her. One of them felt a little heavier than the others. She saved it till last.

The first contained only a business card–sized piece of thin grey newsprint on which a single sentence had once, apparently long ago, been typed or photocopied. It read,

> We thank you for your interest but regret that your novel does not seem right for our list at this time.
> The Editors

Neither the envelope nor the piece of paper gave any clue as to the identity or affiliation of these "Editors." Nevertheless Laurel put the rejection card aside, to be filed later in the bottom drawer of her filing cabinet, which was euphemistically labeled "Correspondence."

The second envelope held a genuine slip, one full third of a regular sheet of paper. The paper too was heavier—possibly even twenty-four-pound—and hardly translucent at all. But the text on the slip, though longer, was no more encouraging.

Dear Author,

The editorial staff would like to thank you for the opportunity of reading your manuscript(s). Please excuse any delay(s) that may have occured in awaiting this response.

The editors reviewed your work(s) with careful attention and real enjoyment. Unfortunately, however, given the quantity of submissions that they receive, sometimes even quality work must be declined. Ultimately, they did not feel passionately enough about your work(s) to be able to give it the support that it deserves.

They regret that the large number of manuscript(s) that they receive makes it impossible for them to respond to you in a more personal manner or to comment in detail on your work(s). They wish you the best of luck in finding a home for it elsewhere.

There followed an invitation to buy some of the publisher's most popular novels at a discounted price.

Her gaze lingered for a while over the words "real enjoyment," but finally drifted contemptuously to the typo in the first paragraph ("occured"), the passive voice in the second, and the solecism in the last ("manuscript(s)"). These should perhaps have cheered her up, but did not: Although it is no dishonor to be criticized by the ignorant, it is depressing to be rejected by them.

The third envelope contained one full, uncut sheet of paper. Fastidiously she unfolded it and smoothed it flat upon the desktop. From her expression, it would have been difficult to pinpoint the moment at which she read the familiar words, "Although we read your manuscript thoroughly and with careful attention, we regret..." She stared at the page for a long time, her eyes roving across it seemingly at random. The text was identical in substance, and in places identical in phrasing, to countless other pieces of correspondence she had received over the years; long familiarity had rendered her snow-blind to this sort of letter. At length she focused on the signature, and discovered that this one was unique after all: it had been signed by hand, in real ink. The name itself was illegible, but the complimentary close read, "Thanks for thinking of us." Also the word "author" in the salutation had been crossed out, and her name (or one very much like it) had been written above.

She ran her fingertips over the handwritten words; she closed her eyes and felt the indentations the pen had made in the page.

Then she filed it away with the others.

She returned to her desk and withdrew from a drawer a notepad and a fat pen. She sat staring out the window for half an hour at the brownstone apartment block across the street. She sighed heavily; then she began to write.

She wrote hunched over her desk, her tongue clamped between her teeth; she wrote quickly and steadily, never pausing to find the right word or consider a character's motives; and she wrote for hours. It has been said that we read to forget ourselves, but that when we write, we have only ourselves to find. I think that Laurel Peggery wrote to forget herself.

She was interrupted that evening by the phone. It took her a moment to recognize the sound; then she lunged across the room—but drew up short, finally lifting the receiver with a shrug of indifference that was not entirely convincing.

"Yeah?"

It was her sister, Vivian. "Have you eaten?"

Laurel gasped irritably. "Is that all you called for?"

"As a matter of fact, Marcel and I were thinking about going to a party."

Laurel said nothing.

"Well, do you want to come?"

Laurel sat down at her desk and stared out the window. After a moment she sighed and said, "I suppose this is just another way of asking if I've eaten?"

"Huh?"

"Or asking in your sly way if I need any help paying the rent? Or whether I ever think about moving into a nicer, larger, sunnier apartment? Or—"

"Where's all this coming from?"

"You're worried about me: that I'm not getting enough social interaction—is that it?"

"I—we—*I* merely thought that you might like to meet some new people."

Laurel stood up. "Well, let me tell you something." She spoke with quiet ferocity. "I don't need any help meeting people. In fact, I—" She cast a wild glance around the apartment, then extended her free arm in a gesture of exasperation or resolve. "I just don't need any help meeting people. I'm not a charity case."

"Okay okay. If you don't want to come, you don't want to come. Sheesh."

After a pause, Laurel said, "I certainly do not."

"All right all right. But hey listen: if you don't want to come to the party—will you come over and babysit?"

Laurel took a step backwards. "I suppose that's the real reason you called!"

Vivian tried for several minutes to convince her otherwise, but Laurel was intransigent.

"You didn't want me to come at all! You knew I'd say no!"

"To be honest, I thought you might. But I always hope you won't."

"Well, Vivian, I'm sorry to disappoint you, but I have changed my mind. You'll just have to find another babysitter."

"Huh? You're coming to the party now?"

"Certainly I am coming."

"That's great," said her sister wearily. Then, plucking up her enthusiasm, she said, "We'll pick you up at nine."

"I shall expect you at ten."

ANGEL SWEPT THROUGH THE PARTY like a breeze stirring piles of leaves. She tried on people's hats and eyeglasses. She asked one man what he was drinking, and without waiting for a reply dipped her finger in his glass and tasted her finger. "Delicious." She elbowed her way into conversations, which she listened to for five seconds, then summed up in one provocatively naive phrase: "But you can't fit all that money in one bank," or "University is for saps," or "Jewish boys are yummy." Her proclamations were as unanswerable as insults, and satisfied by the silence they left in their wake, she flounced on to her next group of victims. Within two minutes of her arrival, every man at the party was keenly aware of her presence, and every woman was keenly aware of their awareness.

Lionel, too embarrassed to break uninvited into other people's discussions, yet terrified of being left alone, followed Angel around the apartment at a distance of six feet, his eyes fixed on the back of her head. He tried to look absorbed and contented so that no one would talk to him; but his discomfort was as manifest as a bad smell, and he wriggled and grimaced and clenched his fists like someone suppressing murderous urges. So no one talked to him.

"I'm sick of you gibing my heels," Angel told him at last. "Go, meet some nice boys and girls." She made shooing gestures, which Lionel fended off like blows.

"I don't want to leave you." He took a deep breath and let it out in a quavering moan. "I—*love* you."

"Can it with that crap." She looked around to make sure no one had heard him, then gave him a light, almost affectionate slap on the mouth. "How many times do I have to tell you?"

"I can't help it," he said, his head, shoulders, and spine drooping under the weight of his shame. "I wish I could but I can't. That's just the way it is."

"So what do you got to keep telling me it for? Look," she said. She grasped him by the arms and twisted him around by the torso, his feet remaining sunk in the carpet as if in mud.

"Where," he said, without looking up.

"Over there. That chickie-poo's been standing all by her lonesome since we got here. Go cheer her up."

Lionel shuddered at the idea. And indeed Laurel Peggery looked intimidating, standing at full height against the far wall, arms crossed, eyebrows raised in sarcastic expectation.

"I can't," he said. "She wouldn't want to talk to me. I'm not interesting. I wouldn't have anything to say."

"Lioney," said Angel in her saccharine, self-pitying voice. "You do like me a little, don't you?"

Lionel simpered like jelly.

"Then give me a kiss," she said, giving him one, hard, on the lips, "and go say hello to that stuck-up bitch." Then she shoved him clear across the room. He collided with Laurel at a gallop, his forehead and her chin coming together with an audible crack.

"I'm so sorry," he cried. "I must have tripped. Are you all right?"

Laurel, after recovering some of her poise, said, "Certainly I am all right."

"I'm really just so, so, so, so, so, so, *so*, SO, *SO* sorry."

"Don't worry about it."

"Are you sure your chin isn't hurt? My head is *throbbing*."
And indeed there were tears in his eyes.

Laurel stopped rubbing her chin, which was glowing red.
"My chin is fine, thank you."

There was a long pause, in which Lionel opened and
closed his mouth like a fish and Laurel examined the backs
of her hands.

"It's a good thing you're so tall," Lionel finally blurted, "or
I might have broken your nose."

Laurel drew herself up to her full stature as if she had
been insulted. "I am not so extraordinarily tall. In fact I'm
hardly above average for my body type."

Lionel blushed and began blinking rapidly at this allu-
sion to her body, which he found majestic and awe-inspiring
in its dimensions.

"I, I, I," he said in three different intonations, then
cleared his throat and tried again: "That is, I meant to say, I,
I, I—I'm the one who's so short."

Laurel never met with agreement without feeling pla-
cated, so she argued reflexively, "You're not exactly tiny."

Lionel would have liked to escape this conversation.
Normally he was adept at escaping conversations: the slightest
distraction, or lapse in the other person's attention, provided
him with all the excuse he needed to unburden the other of his
tiresome presence. Even when in the dentist's chair or splayed
on an operating table, the moment the talk deviated from his
particular case he would offer to come back at a better time.
But Laurel's beseeching gaze never left him, and pinned him to
the spot, writhing like an insufficiently etherized insect. Since
he could not escape, he sought desperately some justification
for standing there, taking up her time.

After many syllables that did not contribute intelligibly
to his meaning, he said at last, "I saw you standing over here

by yourself and I thought, gee, there's someone who's not having much fun either."

"Certainly I am having fun," said Laurel devoutly.

Lionel wilted and said, "Oh."

After another minute of anguished, ringing silence, Laurel said airily, "I would hate to think you came over here to talk to me just because you felt sorry for me."

"Oh, no! No no! It's just that you were by yourself, and..."

"I came with my sister and her husband, but they have wandered off somewhere."

"Oh!" cried Lionel, clutching at this chance. "We should go find them!"

Laurel shook her head. "They'll wander back." Then she prepared herself for a disclosure by adjusting her posture. "To be honest, I get quite enough of them as it is. And since I didn't relish the prospect of following them around like a child or a dog, or of being thrust upon their casual acquaintances like a visiting yokel cousin, I remained behind, here. After all," she said, and looked challengingly at Lionel, "I'm quite capable of introducing myself."

He did not however take the cue and invite her to do so. His thoughts were following a different path. "Then you did not come with—your boyfriend?"

"I most certainly did not. I do not have a boyfriend."

Now he understood. His face flushed with sentiment and he sighed, "Then you're shy too!"

Laurel balked. "Certainly I am not shy!"

Lionel dissolved into an upright puddle of despair. "I'm so sorry. When you're shy, like I am, you start to imagine that everyone else must be shy too. I am very sorry."

The abjectness of his apology nearly made Laurel smile. "It's not so horrible as all that. It's nothing to apologize for. I mean, being shy isn't so bad. It doesn't hurt anyone—no one but yourself, anyway. It's like riding a bicycle in traffic."

"Oh, but you *can* hurt others cycling in traffic! Cars swerve to avoid you and crash into telephone poles. Or they run you over and damage their undercarriage. Or they send you to the hospital and feel terrible all week."

"Are we still talking about shyness?"

"No," Lionel admitted—then reconsidered. "Well, yes! There's nothing more dangerous, more disastrous, than a shy person let loose in a room full of people. Your awkwardness makes others feel awkward. Your embarrassment makes everyone embarrassed for you. The sight of your self-consciousness, as raw as an open wound, makes everybody handle you self-consciously. No one can be honest, no one dares be blunt. That's the worst part: your uneasiness gets in the way of your words, your behavior, your personality, so that on top of everything else you feel like a liar. Shyness is a toxic spill, spreading uneasiness and dishonesty, contaminating everything it comes in contact with. Oh, it's vile!"

While Lionel trembled with humiliation at his outburst, Laurel considered the truth of it. At length she asked, almost shyly, "What made you think *I* was shy?"

Lionel turned his head away from his mistake like a baby turning away from an unpalatable food. "Oh, who knows? A beautiful woman—standing alone—no boyfriend—"

Laurel's face became very still and very grave. She had never in her waking life been called beautiful. Was he flirting with her? Was he teasing? She glared at him, intimating the consequences of toying with her emotions.

Lionel sensed that he had made another error, and apologized. "I'm a fool. I don't know what I'm saying. Pay no attention to me."

"You speak very—cavalierly," said Laurel.

"I know," he moaned. "I never think before I speak. I'm so nervous I just blurt out whatever idiocy comes into my head. It's awful. I'm awful."

"Yes—I suppose that was just a piece of 'idiocy.'"

"Oh, definitely!"

Laurel's mouth moved speechlessly for a moment. "'Definitely'!"

Lionel was completely bewildered. "Well, sure it was. It was just a mistake."

"Then you did not mean it at all when you said that I was ... that I was—"

"Shy? No!" He moved the sweat around on his face with a sweaty sleeve. "Heck no. It was a mistake."

"I wasn't talking about that."

"You weren't?"

"No."

He peered at her timorously. "What were you talking about?"

"I was talking about something else."

"You were?"

"Something else you said."

"Something *I* said?"

Laurel snorted. "I suppose you don't even remember."

"I don't," he confessed. "I don't remember. Sometimes I don't even remember what I've said. Sometimes I don't even hear myself. I don't hear myself and I don't hear the other person, either. I don't hear anything and I sure don't know what I'm saying half the time."

"That's what I figured. You spoke carelessly."

"Boy, you could say that!"

"In that case, I will not hold you to it."

"Gee," he said, "I appreciate that." His posture was that of a man who had just been chased for a mile by wolves. His exhaustion briefly overwhelmed his fear of offending, and he looked around with candid desperation for Angel.

"I see that I am keeping you from your—friend," said Laurel.

"No, not really." He had spotted Angel across the room, draped over a giggling young man whose ears she was cleaning with her tongue.

Lionel's despondence and wistfulness were too much for Laurel's pride. "I hear my sister calling. Goodbye."

"Goodbye," he said softly, long after she had left the room.

WHEN LAUREL WAS A GIRL, she had been ashamed to show her feelings. When it came time for her friends or cousins to go home after a visit, she would go behind the house and scrape her knee on the stucco so that she could cry openly and without embarrassment. That night, after she arrived home, she went into the bathroom and stubbed her toe repeatedly on the corner of the washstand till the toenail split. She sat on the edge of her bed and wept silently for ten minutes. Then she pulled herself upright, bandaged her toe, washed her face with cold water, and sat down at her desk, where she wrote late into the night.

Lionel left the party shortly after Laurel. He wandered the empty streets in aimless dejection. Soon he was lost. He was glad to be lost; he deserved to be lost; he began positively to wallow in his lostness, and turned down obscure streets and narrow, unmarked alleys. Finally he came to a dead end, where a brick wall sealed off the passage. He sighed profoundly, almost sensually, pleased to have this final confirmation of the universe's utter disdain for him. He was about to turn and go when his eye detected the shape of a door in the shadow of the wall. He stepped nearer.

There was indeed a door here, where there could be no need of one. Why should someone wall up an alley only to install a door in the wall? The door was incongruous in its appearance too. It was made of a heavy, lacquered wood, and its surface had been elaborately carved. It was the door to the inner chambers of a judge or to the library in an old mansion, not the sort of door that connected one dirty alleyway to another. The knob was warm to the touch. He turned it.

When Lionel was a boy, he had had an imaginary fairy friend who told him that he was a changeling. However, when Lionel tried to return to Fairyland with him, his friend had informed him that he was not wanted. "Away with ye, ye blethering gobhawk," he had shouted, and thrown stones. The stones, though imaginary, hurt. Lionel had never seen his friend again.

The door was locked. He jiggled the knob, then slowly retraced his steps. He tried to imagine what he might have found on the other side of the door—and for a while forgot that he was not wanted by the universe. He too, when he arrived home, wrote late into the night.

THE HUNTING PARTY

British Columbia, 1905

SHE RAN AWAY from home with an artist who, when she became pregnant, did what he believed was the responsible thing: he married her, gave up painting, and found a steady job. She never forgave him for this treachery: she had certainly never intended to marry a *bank clerk*. When the child arrived, she did not let her husband hold it, and discouraged him as much as possible from speaking to it. She did not want her baby contaminated by his conformity. She spent his salary with an air of pious reproof, like a medieval pope spending the indulgences of sinners, and surrounded her child with expensive pictures, luxurious music, and the most beautiful calfskin-bound volumes of the best books ever written. Little Lance babbled contentedly in his bassinet when she read him a page of Longfellow. She was sure that he would be a great artist.

She subscribed to the idea of art as self-expression, and this idea guided her parenting. The best way, she believed, to nurture her son's artistic self-expression was to allow and indeed encourage him to do anything he wanted to do, and never to force him to do anything he didn't. Thus she praised (silently) his every rude, cruel, and selfish act as a demonstration of his

77

innovativeness and guts, while she disapproved (silently) of any polite, cooperative, or generous behavior as being merely derivative and toadying. Under this (silent) tutelage, Lance soon proved precocious. He uttered his earliest sentences with poetic incorrectitude, cussed instinctively, and colored outside the lines with the very first crayons she gave him. At the dinner table he belched, spat out whatever did not please his palate, and saw through such empty, arbitrary customs as cutlery and napery. Outside the home he pointed at ugly people and sniffed at smelly people, shat in unconventional locales, and kicked puppies and pulled the ears of kitties. He was a natural-born revolutionary.

She took care to indulge his every whim, certain that it was the Muse stirring in him. When he asked for candy, it was because art must be sweet. When he was bored, she arranged play dates with other boys and girls, because art is a social act. When he threw a tantrum over horseshoes, she sent the boys and girls home, because art is nothing if not the product of solitude and reflection. And when his uncompromising individuality discomfited his teachers, she permitted him to stay home from school, because art must find its own path to the truth.

But as he grew older, his whims dwindled. The things he did not want to do multiplied while the things he did want to do decreased, until as a young man all he wanted to do, it seemed, was sit around in soft chairs in dark rooms and read books. Even this he did listlessly, as if he simply couldn't think of anything better to do. She waited in vain for all this solitude and reflection to bear fruit in the form of a novel or even a poem, but the most she ever caught him writing was a note in the margin of an anthology. When she investigated later, she found that he had jotted one single word, faintly and clumsily, beside one of the greatest stanzas in English poetry. The word was "stupid." The poet was Longfellow.

In desperation she began inviting to dinner journalists, poets, novelists, and other writers. But, when Lance could be persuaded to join them at table, he seemed immune to the charms of the writing life. The rewards of imagination, the pride of craft, the challenge of constantly reinventing oneself, the vagaries of fame, the peccadilloes of publishers, the esoteric mystery of royalties—none of this captured his interest. He sat with his chin sunk upon his chest, staring into his soup with glazed eyes, occasionally letting a deep, sawing sigh cut right through one of the guests' anecdotes.

But one night his head snapped up at the sound of his mother laughing—laughing at *him*. Reconstructing the conversation from subliminal fragments, he determined that they had been talking about the war in South Africa. A large bearded man whom Lance vaguely recognized had recounted comprehensively his participation in that event. Then one of the literary ladies had asked Lance's mother if *he* had been in it. This was the idea she found so humorous.

"Why not?" he demanded. "I was old enough. I might have gone."

"Undoubtedly, dearest. Mummy didn't mean anything by it. It was just the thought of you, in big heavy boots, and carrying a *gun*, with a great big pack on your back, climbing a *hill*—" She was overcome again by mirth.

Lance poured his coffee into his soup, pushed back his chair, got to his feet, and sashayed with dignity from the room and out of the house. He decided to run away from home.

He ran away from home often—once or twice a week, lately. The first time, at age twelve, he'd run away to protest a stomach flu which had prevented him from eating as much chocolate as he would have liked. He'd gone around the side of the house and crouched behind a rhododendron bush for fifteen minutes, till he could be sure that the universe and his mother had noted his disapproval. Since that time his escapes had taken him farther and farther from home. He found them both soothing and stimulating, so that by the time he returned—sometimes as much as three-quarters of an hour later—he could scarcely recall the injustice he had fled. Indeed, these runnings away were the closest he came to adventure outside the pages of a novel. He took care never to retrace his steps, but each time struck out in a different direction, trying his utmost to get lost. Most of the time we see the world as a schematic representation of itself, a sort of life-sized three-dimensional map. It is only in unfamiliar surroundings that we see the world as it really is, not carto-graphically, but pictorially, as a painter or photographer sees it. When Lance ran away from home, he instinctively ran away from the familiar and towards the unknown. When he entered a new park or walked down a strange lane for the first time, he felt that it could be a park or lane anywhere in the world—or in another world altogether.

Tonight he had to walk for twenty minutes before he found a turning he had never taken before. For those twenty minutes he brooded upon his mother's slanderous laughter. She thought he was weak! Unmanly! A sissy! He kicked at a stone in the road, but the stone resisted; and he continued on his way, now with a slight hobble and more outraged than ever. When the throbbing in his foot had subsided, he kicked at a leaf, with more satisfactory results.

"There! *That's* your laughter, Mummy! That's your laugh-ing face!" He imagined himself sitting atop her, and imag-ined her bucking and thrashing beneath him, but to no avail. "Now who's a weakling, hey, Mummy? Now who's laughing?"

Then he realized that he had no idea where he was, and his daydreams went out like a flame deprived of oxygen. He looked around him. A rickety fence separated a row of houses from the road, which sloped downhill past a copse of silver beeches to an open field. A lopsided moon outlined every cloud in the sky. The air was warm and moist and smelled faintly of the ocean. He drank in the night—and strode forward, into the unknown.

When he returned home, twenty-two minutes later, he found the large bearded man in the garden, moistening his lips with a brandy and moistening a cigar with his lips.

"Welcome back."

"Thank you."

"Nice walk?"

"Spiffing."

"Your mother." He held the cigar out to investigate his handiwork. "Says you write."

(Mrs. Chitdin had exaggerated.)

Giggling, Lance arranged himself on a nearby bench like a butler putting away the best china. When he was settled, he said nonchalantly, "I've composed ten novels."

(Mrs. Chitdin would have been surprised to hear it.)

"Guess I could see one?" said the man.

"Hardly! I don't write them *down*."

The man rotated the cigar in his mouth. "You just—make them up. In your head."

Writhing with suppressed giggles, Lance said, "I wouldn't know where else to make them up."

A woman came out of the house and joined them. She slipped her hand inside the large bearded man's elbow and said, "Maury, we promised Beepsie we'd be back at the hotel by nine."

"Lonnie," said the man with devastating patience, "it's not your turn right now. When I'm with someone, I'm with them. And right now, as you can see, I'm with the young man. So go back into the house—and don't act all put out. This is basic kindergarten stuff, doll."

A blush appeared on the woman's face, as if she had been slapped on both cheeks. Without another word, but proclaiming her recalcitrance with every step, she returned to the house.

Lance was impressed. "Is that your wife?"

"One of my little sisters, let's call her."

"Gee." He looked at the large bearded man more carefully. "You were in the war, huh?"

"Parts of it."

"Kill anybody?"

"Oh sure," he grimaced. "But one thing you learn. It's a lot easier to shoot a man than it is to pick up his corpse."

Lance lost interest in this sentence about halfway through. He was on his feet, holding an imaginary rifle at the level of his knees, and spraying the garden with imaginary bullets and real spittle. "P-kow! P-kosh! Take *that*, Mother! Ch-chow! Bakaw bakaw! And *that!*"

"Nowadays," said Maury thoughtfully, "I mostly just shoot deer."

HIS MOTHER HAD BEEN A GREAT BEAUTY. She grew accustomed at a young age to marriage proposals and declarations of love; so that when she met Grant Masterson, who did not express his emotions, she was mystified and intrigued. She soon hectored him into admitting that she was beautiful, but it was several months before he betrayed the depth of his true feelings.

One night he asked almost petulantly, "Don't you ever feel lonely?"

"I don't know. Not really. Maybe sometimes." She laughed, "I get by."

"I'd like to make you feel lonely," he said.

"Hey! That's not nice."

"No. But fair's fair."

She peered at him. "*I* make *you* feel lonely?"

His sullen silence confirmed it.

"Then you love me!" she cried, clapping her hands. She was so delighted to have caught him, to have finally pinned him down, that she agreed when, a moment later, he asked her to marry him.

She died giving birth to their first child. Though marriage had not cured his loneliness, it also hadn't lasted long enough to cure him of his illusions. He still believed she was perfect—and, by dying, she guaranteed that his disappointment would be postponed perpetually. He beatified her memory, and blamed the child for her martyrdom.

He hated Maurice even as a baby. But he was good at hiding his feelings, even from himself, and believed that he merely took a cool-headed, pragmatic approach to parenting. In practice, this meant preventing the boy from doing things he wanted to do, and forcing him to do things he didn't. He believed this was the only way to give his son backbone—and it was evident from an early age that the boy was lacking in backbone. Thus, when the baby cried, his father ignored him till the crying ceased. When the boy complained, his father thrashed him till he cried. If he looked sleepy, his father made him stand in the corner and read aloud (but not loud enough to disturb his father's work) a page of Shakespeare: Dr. Masterson could imagine nothing more tiresome than poetry. If he seemed restless, his father sent him to bed. Since he often seemed lonely, his father prohibited playmates. (Besides, he could not stand children, with their hysterical histrionics, like a troupe of clowns desperately faking merriment under threat of the guillotine.

Dr. Masterson prohibited merriment.) If the boy betrayed hunger, his father devised some reason for supper to be delayed, and when the boy looked sated, his father made him clear his plate. First desserts then fruit were outlawed, for Maurice consumed them with too overt pleasure; eventually the boy's diet was restricted to liver, rye bread, and garbanzo beans—the three foods he had shown the most distaste for, before he learned to hide his distastes.

As a man of science and his son's only tutor, Dr. Masterson could not quite bring himself to forbid the boy to read, though Maurice showed hardly any disinclination for this activity. Instead, he waited till the boy appeared most engrossed in a book, then ordered him out of doors to gulp down some fresh air. Occasionally Maurice returned from his exile looking inadequately dispirited, and his father accused him of meeting with other children or of eating an apple. But Maurice assured him that he had done nothing but trudge through the woods—he showed him the mud on his boots—and this satisfied his father, who could imagine no less congenial spot than a tangle of sappy trees beneath a grey, cloud-scoured sky.

His son felt differently, but was wise enough to keep this a secret.

One day, however, he brought home a bird with a broken wing, and his father inferred the truth. The boy's imagination had made the wood a refuge, and peopled it with animal friends. This had to be stopped.

"You mustn't interfere with Nature," he admonished. "The fit survive, and the unfit—die."

"But couldn't we mend his wing? Then he would be fit again."

Dr. Masterson shook his head ponderously. "If he didn't die of shame, he'd be eaten alive by the other birds. He's got the human smell on him now. They'd take him for an outsider."

The boy looked aghast at his own arms, as if expecting to see the human stench rising from them.

"No," continued his father, "the only legitimate reason to kidnap a wild animal from its natural environment is the scientific one: vivisection. If you like, we could pin this fellow down in my laboratory and cut him open to see how his insides work."

The boy went pale.

"Otherwise, there remains only the *humane* approach," said the doctor with a sneer in his voice. "If you will not use a broken, suffering animal for the advancement of knowledge, then you must put it out of its misery. Wasteful, I call it—but it's the least you can do."

So, in the end, Maury carried the bird out to the road and dropped a rock on it.

"*HUNTING?*" MRS. CHITDIN DID NOT like the idea at all. Wasn't it dangerous? Mr. Masterson assured her the only critters that would bite a man holding a .490 Winchester Express were wood ticks and frost. The trip would be good for Lance, would toughen him up, would put some sap in his branches. Mrs. Chitdin wasn't so sure: Could one harden butter? But Lance was so insistent that she felt it could only be the Muse urging him on. Perhaps there would be a novel in it, after all. So, the following week, she packed his trunks, fed him breakfast, dressed him warmly, and drove him to the train station.

The men reached the end of the line mid-afternoon. Maury went in search of a couple of gillies to take down their luggage, first warning Lance not to attempt this himself: "An Indian'll only do what he thinks you can't." This warning was somewhat superfluous, since Lance had seventeen trunks, none of which he could lift even the handles of. And he was deliriously fatigued from the train ride, which had already lasted longer than the entire hunting trip had lasted in his imagination.

By the time Maury returned, Lance had sprawled out on the platform and fallen into a light doze; the rail crew had piled his and Maury's luggage around his body, and the train had pulled out again, back to the coast and the comforts of civilization.

"I think I've got a stiff shoulder," said Lance ominously.

But the expedition faced even greater problems. The two Indians whom Maury had brought back with him—visibly against their will—claimed to be unable to carry seventeen trunks and eight heavy canvas packs by themselves without horses. They also claimed to be unable to speak English.

"Hay-lo wa-wa King George."

"They bloody do so wa-wa King George," said Maury affably. "They're just too lazy to bother. And this way, when they don't want to do something, they can pretend not to understand and just sit around growing hair. Isn't that right, Rocky?"

The one called Rocky shrugged, as if to say he could see Maury's point but wanted to hear other opinions on the matter.

It was decided, through a largely one-sided exchange of gestures and wa-wa, that Old Moose would go with Maury to buy pack ponies from one of the ranches, and Rocky would stay behind with Lance to watch the gear. Old Moose looked back wistfully at the younger men, who were already pushing the bags together into a makeshift cot.

In the end, however, even five ornery-looking ponies, one Rocky, and one Old Moose were unequal to Lance's trunks. For the first time, Maury paused to wonder what all Lance had brought with him. Lance didn't know, and was just as curious. "Let's take a boo!" he suggested, but did not stir from his couch. So Maury rifled through his belongings, holding up items for him to see, identify, and justify or discard.

"Those are my sleeping gowns. I need those. I sleep."

"Lend you a pair of my pyjamas. And these things?"

"Oh good—my butter paddles. Did she pack my butter too? I can't endure the salted."

"Got all the food we'll need, and you can use a knife and a billy like the rest of us. This gizmo?"

"My police rattle."

"No police where we're going, son. And this?"

"Oo, I should have that on. That's my cholera belt."

"Cripes! There's no cholera in the Cariboo!... Now what on God's green earth do you need a dull old knife for?"

"That's a book knife, you silly. It *has* to be dull, or you're liable to cut your fingers on the pages."

"Use the back of my filleting knife. —What the hell am I talking about? You brought *books*?"

"Just Meredith."

Maury rummaged around in the trunks. "The Life and Works of Lord Macaulay, Complete in Ten Volumes!?"

"Oh, Lord. I *distinctly* told her Meredith. I can't read *history* on a hunting trip."

The Indians, however, seemed to admire Lance's sleeping gowns and the lifework of the British essayist in ten volumes, so Maury struck a deal with them: They would be paid in advance for their services as guides with the extra chattels, which in the meantime would remain with the stationmaster for safekeeping. Lance, who was at that moment daydreaming about wrestling a panther, offered no objection.

By this time it was dusk, and too late even to inquire about a hotel. In any case, the town of Quesnel Arm seemed to consist altogether of the train station, a dry goods store, and eleven clapboard cabins facing eleven directions, like misanthropes huddling together for warmth. Rocky made a suggestion.

"Ni-ka house moo-sum po-lak-le."

Maury grunted; looked left; spat; looked right; and grunted again. "Well, let's see it."

Rocky's house was on the river, which they were able to find in the dark by its stench. It was late in the spawning season, Maury explained, and the salmon, having struggled heroically upstream to lay their eggs as high in the mountains as possible—leaping boulders, hurling themselves from puddle to puddle, swimming against rapids and even up waterfalls—had now given up the fight, and let the river carry them where it would, to be smashed on rocks, grated like cheese on riverbeds, washed ashore, and scooped up by bears, ranchers with pitchforks, and Indians. "It's shooting ducks in Central Park. It's not hunting; it's not even fishing; it's harvesting." He'd seen spots where the riverbanks consisted entirely of a crunchy white sand: the powdered, sun-bleached bones of salmon. The stench coming from the river was dead salmon rotting in the shallows faster than the Indians could eat or smoke them.

Lance gagged. "How can they stand it?"

"Oh, they don't even notice it. The Indian's sense of smell is much less acute than the white man's."

Lance peered thoughtfully at Rocky's nose, while fingering his own.

Rocky's house—which turned out also to be Old Moose's house, and the house of several other men and women and innumerable children of all ages—seemed to corroborate Maury's claim. Surely no one with a working nose could live in such a place. A fire burned somewhere, or perhaps smoldered universally under the heaps of oily rags and children, filling the air with an acrid smoke that instantly coated the lungs and sinuses. A horrific chandelier of gutted salmon carcasses hung from the rafters, infusing the smoke almost visibly with an odor of seafood and putrefaction. Mixed with this overpowering stink were several merely unpleasant smells: kerosene, rancid lard, pine needles, stale sweat, fresh sweat, rich dirt, diapers, and milk.

"Ni-ka house," said Rocky, with blasé pride.

Maury was about to say that they couldn't possibly stay in such a squalid hovel; but seeing Lance gasping and teetering and about to swoon, he declared that it was a grand house, and that they would be honored to spend the night in it. Lance collapsed onto a pile of rags and squealing babies. One of the women placed in his hands a bowl of fish parts swimming with some of their former spawning-season tenacity in a black broth. Without thinking, he thanked her, and this reflex of etiquette sealed his fate: to run screaming back to the train station no longer seemed possible. With a whimpering giggle, he resigned himself to a night of voluptuous misery.

But the night would not let him wallow in his unhappiness. After the lamps were put out, he detected a thin draught of fresh outdoor air, but this kept moving, and he had to move with it, clambering over sleeping bodies that merely grunted when he put a knee in their groin or a thumb in their eye. Some of the children, fascinated by his white hair, pointy nose, squeaky droning voice, and total lack of good manners, followed him in his migrations; and whenever he had enough temporary warmth and breathable air to doze off, one of the children would begin playing with his face, sniffing his clothes, or tasting his hair. By the time they fell asleep, they had learned several new King George cuss words. But after the fidgeting and murmuring of the children ceased, Lance became aware of other strange sounds and fleeting movements in the darkness. Something, not a draught, passed over his foot; then something, not a child, brushed his ear. He was utterly awake, and utterly alone in his wakefulness. He wanted to shake one of the children, but could not move. Terror filled his lungs—then burst out in a warbling shriek when something with tiny claws and a long sleek tail scurried across his face. He sprang to his feet without passing through any intermediate position and stayed as much off the ground as possible by hopping from one big toe to the other and flapping his arms for extra lift. A tremendous commotion ensued. Lamps were lit, blankets thrown off, sticks and pans and rags grabbed as weapons, and there arose from the entire household the war cry of "Tsish-o-poots! Tsish-o-poots!"

Maury rolled over, and not realizing that Lance had moved across the room, explained sleepily that Indians hated porcupines and considered them evil because they liked to chew out the brake cables from the undercarriage of automobiles. "But a porcupine doesn't know any damn better. It's just the salt we put on the roads that he likes." He rolled over again, and, disgusted, fell back asleep.

In the morning, Lance was too tired to realize fully what indignities and discomforts he was being subjected to. He was prodded upright, stuffed with fish, irrigated with coffee, somehow insinuated into wool socks, wool underwear, flannel shirt, sweater, gabardine jacket, hip waders, trench socks, puttees, boots, gaiters, mackinaw overcoat, and several hats, and set marching on a trail through the forest before he knew what was happening to him. He kept seeing porcupines at the edge of his vision, and could feel them nibbling at his hair. When at last he awoke to his surroundings, he made a stand—literally. Planting his feet in the mud, he declared that he would go no farther, that he had gone far enough.

Maury squinted up through the trees at the dark blue clouds, and said that he understood. Not everyone was cut out for the sportsman's life. "It can be glorious, and it can be rough. And mostly, I guess, it's rough. Well, your mother'll be glad to see you back so soon. So long, old son. Rocky, Old Moose: Kla-ta-wa."

"But—but I can't go back *alone!*"

Maury squinted at him as if he were a dark blue cloud. "Why?"

"Because! Because I don't know the way! Because it's not even light out! Because I'm wearing your clothes! *Because!*"

"Oh, send the jacket and things over to the Esquire. Guess I'm bound to drop in there again someday."

Lance abandoned all pretense. "What about *panthers!*"

Maury said that the North American panther, or puma, or catamount, or cougar, or mountain lion, or Californian lion as he was sometimes called in Washington State, or hy-as puss-puss (big puss-puss) as the Indians called him, was a shifty, gutless cur who'd sneak and skulk after you for miles, howling like a street cat in heat, but would hardly ever show fight directly, and had almost never been known to attack a man unprovoked.

Lance decided that he would stay with the hunting party a little longer.

The clouds overhead changed from blue to grey and slowly filled with light, till the whole sky seemed a dull, diffuse sun. Rain did not fall so much as hang in the air in microscopic droplets, so that Lance, looking back, thought he could see the path they had cut through it. Farther on, the trees traded their leaves for needles and shaggy filaments that bristled with damp. Everything was damp and musty, like old potatoes left too long in a cellar. All the rocks, ferns, and fallen logs were spattered with a grey-blue moss like mold, and the tops of the trees were white with mildew. As the trail stretched uphill, Lance was soon wheezing, but he blamed this on the air. He imagined he could feel tiny grains, like infinitesimal spores, when he inhaled. He coughed and spat till he was completely out of breath, certain that he had acquired tuberculosis, developed several new allergies, and caught a bad cold. When they paused to let the ponies graze, the symptoms abated too much for him to raise an alarm; and when they set out again he was soon too winded to speak. This was life, he thought: a cheerless footslog towards death that left you too breathless to protest.

Maury, however, had breath to spare. To him the forest smelled fresh, and the damp affected him like wine. He gave Lance the Latin and common names of the flora around them, and told him of the habits and character of the fauna that were at present nowhere to be seen. He gave the dimensions of the mountains on the horizon and explained the origin of the region's name. There had been a time when caribou had swarmed over these mountains like ants on a carcass, when a man could shoot a hundred in a single season with a single gun. But then had come the commercial hunters. Maury's face furrowed with contempt. A man would kill anything anyhow if his sole aim was to sell it. He'd still-hunt in rainy season, burn down the forest in dry season, draw out stags with a cheap birch-bark horn in rutting season. He'd even stoop to trapping. And caribou had a fatal idiosyncrasy: at the sound of a gunshot, they would freeze. An unscrupulous hunter—a commercial hunter—could, as long as he stayed downwind, slaughter an entire herd with a single gun.

Lance asked when they were going to shoot something. His feet were sore.

Maury cleared his throat, sniffed the air, and spat. "When we're off the beaten path, little brother. Anything still alive around here only comes out at night."

Lance pointed at something moving in the branches overhead. "What about that?"

"That," said Maury, "is a squirrel."

Lance shuddered; he hated squirrels. "Well, let's shoot it."

"With an Express? There'd be nothing left."

Lance did not understand the objection. He pointed again. "There. Shoot that guy."

"Christ on a stick. That's a snowy owl."

"So?"

"You don't shoot owls."

"Why not? He's just sitting there." He had the feeling that the owl was watching him; he lowered his voice. "Go on, get him."

Rocky and Old Moose came forward and joined the discussion, nodding and pointing illustratively with their guns and encouraging Maury to give it a try.

"Hy-as gun. Ten-as kula-kula. Klo-she ma-mook poh. Easy bang-bang."

"You don't shoot owls," Maury grumbled. "Owls are hunters. You don't shoot hunters."

Rocky's gun went off. Lance and Maury jumped; the owl flapped its wings, but did not fall or fly away. The shot had gone wide, or had only been intended to demonstrate the convenient operation of the trigger.

"You damn idiot." Maury yanked the rifle from Rocky's hands. "Shut the hell up and get the hell back, goddamn you."

When they had retreated as far as the pack train, Maury turned to the owl, held the gun up over his head, and threw it ostentatiously to the ground. The owl ruffled its feathers and blinked. Then Maury began to speak to it, in a low, soothing, clucking voice. Lance could not make out the words, but the owl seemed to understand perfectly, and to be rather impressed by what he heard. He emitted an inquisitive hoot, and hopped to a lower branch to better hear the reply. Maury held out his hands and took a step forward. The owl blinked, ruffled its feathers, and cocked its head. Then, to the amazement of Lance and the Indians, it lifted itself from its perch and floated down into Maury's open hands.

"What's he doing?," Lance whispered. His view was blocked by Maury's back.

When Maury turned around, the owl had disappeared. In its place there remained only a limp clump of feathers, which Maury tossed aside like an old newspaper.

"Kla-ta-wa," he said, and continued up the trail.

Lance and the Indians were in raptures. Again and again they reenacted the seduction, the capture, the brutal murder. Shooting wasn't cruel enough for this man; he preferred to strangle his prey with his own hands! What a man! What a monster!

It was not till they stopped for lunch that Lance noticed the blood on Maury's hands. Rocky's shot had grazed the owl after all.

WHILE THE INDIANS MADE CAMP, Lance sat bored and shivering on a rotten stump, watching Maury build a fire. Maury had not spoken much since that morning, but now could not resist the opportunity to instruct.

"Cedar deadfall is no damn good," he said. "Holds the water too deep. Pine will do in a pinch. But fir is your best bet. You can see the difference in the grain. Pine's more porous."

Lance grimaced, his jaw too clenched from cold to permit a yawn.

Maury placed a log on end in the mud, balancing it for a moment with one finger; then, before it could tip over, he brought the hand-axe down in four powerful strokes, reducing a gnarled piece of tree to a perfectly smooth and rectangular stick of lumber about one twentieth its original size. When he had made thirty or so of these, he constructed a little tapering log cabin and stuffed it with paper from a waterproof tin. He then struck a match, and pausing conclusively, like a math teacher drawing a line under the figures to be summed, lit the paper. It burned magnificently, brightly and quickly, and left no trace. Only the log cabin remained, steaming slightly but otherwise intact.

Maury gave a grunt of satisfaction and explained that now the surface moisture had been burned off. He added and lit more paper, with the same results.

Evidently the region had received more rain than had been reported. Well, even a cold supper would taste good after a day's hard hiking.

Suddenly the little log cabin burst into flame. Rocky had doused it with a liter of lantern oil, and now stood admiring his handiwork and basking in his employers' unequal gratitude.

That night Maury—sitting before the fire that Rocky had started, eating the salmon that Old Moose had cooked, and drinking the blackberry wine that their wives had fermented—complained about the laziness, uncleanliness, and unpreparedness of Indians. What were they doing with lantern oil and blackberry wine, when they had not brought tents or sleeping outfits or boots? They had signed on to the expedition without even asking how long they were to be gone or where they would be going. He called that sheer suicidal stupidity. And they had lice that they didn't scratch. They didn't even mind. They were *proud* of their lice!

Lance, lying curled around the fire, paid no attention to this diatribe, but listened instead to the Indians laughing and reminiscing about their exploits. Having never learned any language other than English, and having acquired that without much difficulty, he was unsurprised to discover that he understood their language perfectly—just as long as he did not concentrate too hard. It helped perhaps that their jargon had borrowed several words from English; and from such hints as "bed," "house," "shoes," "sick," and "gun," eked out with the Indians' dramatic gestures and his own dramatic imagination, he was easily able to piece together their story. It seemed that Old Moose had been, as a young Moose, something of a rake and a daredevil. He would face any danger, perform any stunt, if a girl was nearby. One time, spurred on by the most beautiful girl in the village, he had climbed a tree to a panther's nest, and with his own two hands—

"What a load of horse crap," said Maury, staggering to his feet. "If a bear lets you crawl into his *den*, and take aim by his *breath*, and blast him in the *dark*, it's because he's hibernating—that's all there is to it. I don't care what you say. That's not hunting, that's murder." Turning to Lance, he said, "They don't hunt, they murder. They only eat the heart, the lungs, and the liver, then they sell the pelt to the Boston man and leave the rest rotting on the ground. I knew a Siwash whose brother was killed by a bear, so he went and killed six of them in revenge, and left their carcasses putrefying in the sun—as a *warning*. As if a bear understands revenge! As if a bear understands your warnings!" He sat back down, muttering that it was a damn waste.

"When are we going to shoot some bears?," Lance wanted to know.

Maury spat into the fire and said nothing for a minute. "Rocky! Pot-latch gun-gun!"

Rocky went to fetch the guns. Lance sat up, giggling.

"Before you can shoot a bear," said Maury proverbially, "you have to learn to shoot. Now, a good gun is a good gun.

This Express, for instance, puts their rusty old smooth-bore muskets to the blush. But even a lousy gun will shoot true within its ability if taken care of, and even a good gun will fail you if you fail it. Improper maintenance is the cause of most misfirings." He brooded for a moment over the death of the owl; then said, "I'll show you how to avoid that."

Lance sighed and lay back down. "Maybe later. I'm comfortable right now," he lied.

He stared into the fire, dreaming of the most beautiful girl in the village, while Maury explained the importance of testing your cartridges in the chambers each morning; the indispensability of extra hammers, mainsprings, and tumbler pins; and above all the necessity of regular and thorough oiling.

The Indians watched in amazement as Maury disassembled the gorgeous shooting stick and rubbed its parts with magic ointment. They could not understand how such a stupid man had built such a wonderful tool.

Lance did not sleep well that night either. As soon as he closed his eyes, the forest came alive, crackling with movement. Small rustling sounds made him think of rats and porcupines and little burrowing creatures with protuberant teeth and piercing red eyes; large intermittent sounds made him think of lions and bears and hulking muscular predators with razor-sharp claws and noses powerful enough to smell the meat under his skin. Instead of protecting him, the tent trapped him, depriving him of sight and preventing escape. He lay rigid and sweating as a panther came towards him with infinite patience, one step a minute; he heard it reach out and hook its index claw into the top clasp of the tent's outer fly—

The sight of Lance the next morning filled Maury with pity and contempt. To assuage his pity, he let him ride atop one of the pack ponies' loads; to assuage his contempt, he lectured him on the importance of self-discipline in the production of literature.

"If I waited for inspiration to strike, I'd still be writing my first novel. Hell—I'd still be writing my first paragraph."

Lance, splayed limply across the swaying mountain of equipment, mumbled that no amount of effort or strain could produce a single beautiful idea or one lovely phrase. "Otherwise athletes and energetic businessmen would write the best novels."

Maury argued that they very well might, if they applied themselves wholeheartedly to the task. He admitted that all writing had an unconscious component; occasionally one surprised oneself. But this was not a passive process. In order to see Paris, one must leave the hotel. In order to find a bridge, one must walk along the river—sometimes for miles.

Lance bleated derisively. "Miles and miles of tedious filler! Flailing about for something to say! Drowning in ink—and taking your reader down with you!"

"Once you've found the bridge," said Maury, "you can go back and cover your tracks." He slapped down a qualm. "Besides, you can't just cross bridges all day."

Lance looked down pityingly at the top of his head. "I'm afraid that you are too old for me to be able to help you."

Maury grunted. "The Muse helps those who help themselves."

Before Lance could reply, he was thrown to the ground when the pony beneath him stopped dead. He was still absorbing this development when, not far from his head, Maury's gun went off. This threw him into a state of total disorientation which seemed to last a very long time, though in fact it was only a few seconds before he was on his feet and staring at the belly of a grizzly bear.

The bear was in a bad mood, having been poisoned already that morning, and now shot. She did not know that she had been poisoned and shot, of course; at most, she understood that she had eaten some bad meat (a coyote carcass laced with arsenic and intended for the local tsish-o-poots population), and that an unexpected encounter with the noisy, earth-hardening animals had rendered her breathless and frightened. Her fear made her angry. She roared, and clawed the air with her forepaws.

Lance understood that he was about to die. He felt no fear—only a tremendous regret. His life did not flash before his eyes; he realized that continually his life had been flashing before his eyes, and that he had paid no attention, made no effort to grasp it or comprehend it. The strength of his remorse proved that there would be no afterlife. For the first time, he understood that he was his body; and his body understood, for the first time, that it was a unique configuration of matter subject to dispersion and decay.

And yet, for the time being, it continued to draw breath and to circulate blood. There is no stillness in life, only standing waves. No idea, no thought, not even the thought of death, can lodge itself permanently in the brain. Other ideas supplant it. Events supervene. Gradually Lance became aware of Maury's voice. He was speaking to the bear.

"Lay down, old daddy. There's nothing more for you to do. You've done your part, and done it well. Now you can rest. In fact, you're asleep already—you just don't know it yet. That bullet I put in you passed clean through like a needle. Your heart slowed it down a little. Your lungs slowed it down a little. But only the skin on your back could stop it. You're all chewed up inside, brother. You're all done in. Nothing to moan about. You've had your time, that's all. Soon enough we'll have had ours too. You're hurting, I know, but not for long. Three minutes from now, no matter how you play it, you'll be sound asleep. So you might as well take it easy as take it hard. Lay down and die, big daddy. Lay on down and die."

Lance thought Maury was speaking to him, and had almost resigned himself to being eaten, when another gun went off behind him. Old Moose's bullet, it was later discovered, passed miraculously through Lance's armpit, tearing his shirts and jackets to shreds but not so much as scratching his skin, and lodged itself in the bear's throat, just as the grizzly's open mouth was about to come down on Lance's head like a snuffer on a candle. That night at the campfire, Lance had plenty of opportunity to wonder why Maury, instead of standing there sermonizing, hadn't simply reloaded his rifle. The reason, he decided, was that Maury was crazy.

He circled the campfire and planted himself before Maury, his body so rigid with defiance that he was bent backwards. With fists clenched, eyes rolled up to one side, and through lips pursed as tightly as a knot in thread, he requested to be shown their present location on the map; he would find his own way back in the morning. Maury chuckled and philosophized that the danger of maps was that a person tended to see only what was on them. Lance returned stiffly to his side of the fire, then drooped in despair. No map!

He decided to enlist the Indians in his mutiny. But, maddeningly, though he understood them, they could not be made to understand him, no matter how eloquently or emphatically he spoke.

"Chuck-a-luck back-track pronto," he suggested.

They shrugged amicably and offered him the jug of blackberry wine. He slapped it aside, and tried again.

"Ding-a-ling a ping-pong. Zig-zag a bee-bop, big stick to Rocky house at itsy-bitsy sun-time. Chim-a-lim-a-lam-fram-jam, man!"

The Indians shook their heads and pantomimed bewilderment.

"Gah!" It was no use. It was as Maury had said: They pretended not to understand so they wouldn't have to do anything. Lazy degenerates! He was on his own.

He swiped the jug of blackberry wine from Rocky's hands and Maury's gun case from the stump where it lay and withdrew with them to the solitude of his tent, where he got quietly drunk, on his own.

When the first faint glow of dawn began at last to seep into the sky, Lance burst out of the tent and hurled himself down to the river—having waited for this moment most of the night, writhing alternately in agony from a full bladder and in terror of being eaten by a vengeful bear. He put the gun case down just long enough to relieve himself, then snatched it back up and spun around several times to make sure nothing had crept up behind him. He relaxed a little then, and with his back to the river, sat down on a log.

The woods were quiet now; the trees seemed held in place by mist. Only the river burbled behind him. Nothing moved, yet the scene was not still like a photograph, but seemed to quiver with movement too subtle for his eyes. Then a breeze soughed high through the trees, rustling the branches in swirling arabesques like the unfurling of cigarette smoke in a sunny room. For a moment, his personality drained from him as from a sieve; all that remained was the universe listening to itself breathe. Then he felt silly, and headed back to camp.

But camp was not where he had left it. He felt a spasm of doubt and fear: had he come the wrong way? But the river was not more than twenty feet from his tent; he could hardly have got lost in such a short distance. He decided that Maury and the Indians were playing a trick on him.

While he was down at the river, they had moved camp. But when he looked for traces of last night's fire, or holes in the ground where they had picketed the ponies, or the cedars from which they had stripped the boughs for their beds, he could find nothing, no sign whatsoever that the spot had been camped in. Still, the camp must be nearby; he had not travelled far enough to miss it by much. If he stayed parallel to the river, he was sure to find it. So, holding the gun case aloft like a staff to keep the branches and cobwebs out of his face, he pushed his way into the foliage at his right.

He stopped again after only a few feet. He was making too much noise; the bears and panthers could probably hear him miles away. Moving more slowly, but not much more silently, he turned back in the direction of the false camp. If the brush was not thinner on the other side, he would go back down to the river and find the correct path up to camp. But the clearing did not appear when he expected it to, and soon he realized that he was not backtracking at all but blazing a fresh trail. Panic rose in his throat like an air bubble; he swallowed it down. All he had to do was retrace his steps, one at a time, all the way back to the river. But when he turned to look for them, he could not find even the most recent. For all his crashing and hacking and stomping, he appeared not to have broken a single branch or crushed a single fern. He was hemmed in by a wall of dense, supple, virgin forest.

He panicked. He ran gibbering and thrashing through the trees, zigzagging as if dodging bullets. When his foot caught a root, he fell mouth first into a clump of devil's warclub. Five minutes later he was still removing thorns from his lips and gums and nostrils and the moist corners of his eyes—but the pain saved him from flying into total hysteria. He took several quick but deep breaths and surveyed his situation with what felt like heroic honesty and fortitude. He was filthy, yes; he was bruised; he was punctured and bleeding and probably poisoned; he was lost and he was utterly utterly alone—

No, after all there was nothing to be gained by surveying his situation. He got to his feet and began walking at random, humming to drown out honest or fortitudinous thoughts.

Unfortunately, thoughts kept surfacing. The first was that he might be walking in circles—so he walked more quickly, to escape the orbit by centrifugal force. Then it occurred to him that he might be walking straight away from camp, deeper and deeper into the forest—so he walked more slowly. Then he had the idea that he could plot his course by the position of the sun. The only problems with this idea were that it was too early for the sun to be above the trees, that it was too cloudy for the sun to be seen anyway, and that even if he were able to orientate himself, he did not know which direction he should be going.

Then he remembered the river. If he could only find it again, he felt certain that he could follow it back to the campsite. He stood stock-still, a trembling antenna, and listened with all his might for the sound of running water. But all he could hear were the creaking of trees, the swishing of their leaves and the clattering of their branches. When for a moment the wind died down he thought he could hear— yes—*something*. It could be the river! But where? He closed his eyes, clenched his teeth, and squeezed his fists. There! No; there? He twisted his head minutely, homing in on the signal ... A bird began squawking and twittering like a drunken idiot at a boat race; he swore and brandished the gun case at it. Then the wind returned. With a despondent whinny, he set out in the probable direction of the river, stopping and listening again every ten or twenty steps. At times he was sure he heard it; more often he could hear nothing but the infernal racket of the forest. At last he came to doubt that he had ever heard anything. He gave up listening, but trudged on in a straight line till the ground began to slope uphill and he knew that he was going the wrong way. Discouragement flooded through him like fatigue. But wait! If he knew the wrong way, he also knew the right way. All he had to do was keep moving downhill and he must eventually reach the river. Unfortunately, the ground was uneven and it was not easy to tell which direction was more downhill or went further downhill than the others. Eventually he reached a spot where the declivity, interrupted by a ridge, forked in two opposite directions. He went left.

The trees here were very tall and widely spaced, like a colonnade in a cathedral. There was less undergrowth—sunlight must almost never penetrate to the forest floor here—but the ground underfoot was spongy and squishy and impeded his movement. He realized that he was walking on years and years of putrefying leaves and deadfall—that he was slogging, indeed, through a giant midden. Once, as a child, after a heavy snowfall, he had tried to make an igloo out of the cook's scrap heap; but his shovel had produced a living cutaway diagram of the interior, rife with rot and teeming with worms and maggots and beetles and millipedes. Now he imagined swarms of such creatures clinging to his boots like honey to a spoon, and the thought made him gag. He walked faster, or tried to, and nearly fell. After that he walked carefully, his face screwed to one side in disgust at the thought of his fate if he were to stumble here. Probably his skeleton would be picked clean, as if by a school of piranhas, in under a minute.

Then he saw something amazing. A single stalk of green, culminating in a delicate yellow flower like an infolded flame, sprouted from the rotting offal. And then he spotted another, and another. The amazing thing was that they did not look blighted, but perfectly healthy. These plants were *thriving!* He crushed one under his boot in disapproval. But a minute later, when he emerged from the dark cathedral and encountered a thicket of brambles, the lesson was brought home to him. These bright red spiny shrubs shot out in every direction from the tangled nest of last year's dead and dried remains. So it was the same everywhere. The forest fed on itself; the forest grew out of its own corpse. Yuck!

He staggered on, not knowing what else to do. For three nights he had hardly slept; he was so tired he could not even lift his thoughts. The woods closed in on him till he seemed to be clawing his way out of a wet prickly sack. He would have lain down and slept, or died, but there was no place for him to rest so much as a foot without fear of its being nibbled by insects, overgrown with rootlets, or dissolved in ooze. He yearned wretchedly for someplace warm, dry, and soft—even some*thing* warm and dry and soft: a cream bun fresh from the oven, or a single square inch of the carpet by the fireplace in his library—anything to remind him that there was comfort and beauty in the world. Ah, beauty! If only he could hold in his hands for one minute a watercolor by Burne-Jones, or press to his chest for one minute a volume of Meredith's, or nuzzle for one minute a single sheet of Mozart, he might find the strength to carry on.

What he found instead was a stream. He was slowly coming to terms with the unwelcome prospect of having to cross it, when he remembered that he had been looking for a river, once. This one did not seem so large as the one he had sat beside, ages ago, at dawn. But rivers, he understood, were like streets: they intersected. This one should eventually meet the bigger one. But in which direction? His mind provided the answer in the form of an image: He saw a wide swollen river overflowing its banks, like a canteen springing leaks; these offshoots in turn drained into smaller tributaries. So, if he followed this one upstream, he must come to the parent river.

It was not, however, as easy a matter to follow a stream as he had imagined. The forest had no respect for boundaries, and came right down to the edge of the water, and indeed spilled over into the water. He was able to make some progress by swinging the gun case like a machete, and temporarily flattening the largest ferns and saplings by stepping on them at their base. Eventually however he came to a spot where the growth was so dense that he could scarcely peer into it, let alone penetrate it, and he was forced down into the stream itself. The water was not deep, but looked cold and dirty, and he did not trust his boots; so he hopped from slimy rock to slimy rock, snatching at branches and pinwheeling his arms to keep his balance while he calculated the next leap. He was just beginning to marvel at his own dexterity, and almost to enjoy himself, when he slipped.

Without any assistance on his part, his rear foot came nimbly forward and planted itself beneath his slewing center of gravity. He might not even have fallen had his boot come down on flat ground, instead of a rocky, mossy riverbed.

He yelped in pain—then in surprise, then again in self-pity. He had twisted his ankle, possibly broken it. He crawled, on elbows and one knee, out of the stream and into a narrow opening between two entangled bushes, then collapsed blubbering, too hurt and miserable to roll onto his back or lift his face from the mud. When, some time later, a bug crawled across the back of his neck, he did not even slap it away.

Unfortunately, he did not die from his injury, nor from grief; and eventually hunger and thirst goaded him back to life. He wriggled down to the stream again and examined the water. A white froth collected in the slow-moving eddies, but even when he scooped water from the center of the stream in his cupped hands he could see a greenish scum floating on top. He could crudely filter the water through his fingers, leaving the scum behind in his hands, if only he had another receptacle. He looked at the gun case. It too had fallen in the stream, but did not look damp now. And when he removed the rifle and the mesh pouch of cartridges from the interior and placed them on a bed of twigs and leaves, they did not appear to be wet. Perhaps the bag would hold water as well as keep it out. So, placing the open bag between his knees, he trickled water into it through his hands. It was a slow process and his hands were soon numb, but if it spared him malaria or cholera he supposed it was worth the trouble. The end result, however, looked even dirtier and tasted like grease, but he slurped till he had exchanged his thirst for queasiness. He refilled the gun case with water to take with him, tied the cartridge-pouch to his belt, and—using the rifle as a sort of crutch, with the barrel wedged in his armpit so that it would not get clogged with mud—tried to stand.

It was no good. The pain was too much for him; he did not like pain. He could neither put any weight on the injured ankle nor let it dangle in the air. And any movement of any part of his body seemed to entail a complementary movement of his ankle, so that all movement hurt. It was clear that he would not be able to walk—not over this terrain, not for any distance. A sense of his isolation came over him. Though he had realized intellectually that he was "in the middle of nowhere," he had not truly felt it before now. At no point in the journey had he been overwhelmed or awed by the exoticism of his surroundings, perhaps because that exoticism had been achieved gradually, step by tedious step. Even yesterday he would not have been *so* surprised if they had bumped into someone he knew. But now, suddenly, he felt as if he had been dropped into the forest from a balloon—or onto another planet from a spaceship.

"Help," he said, at first without much conviction. "Help. Help me." But each repetition brought with it a little more sincerity, and soon he was shouting, then hollering, then screaming wordlessly till his throat was raw.

The only reply was the incessant chittering of birds.

The trilling of one little finch, half the size of his palm, caught his attention. He watched it call shrilly in one direction, flick its head anxiously to and fro, then hop around on its branch and call in the other direction. He felt its desperation; he shared its fear. And he understood, for the first time, the true purpose of "birdsong," that blithe misnomer. Birds did not sing; they cried for help. This little fellow had obviously been separated from his friends and was begging them to come back. The entire forest resounded with these cries of terror. Nature was not an opera house, but a colossal slaughterhouse.

He remembered what he had supposedly learned yesterday: that he was going to die. But now he could muster no resignation towards this fact. He was not ready to die. He did not want to die. Why should he have to die? His body quailed at the idea, like a dog cringing at the threat of a kick. Even discomfort, even pain was preferable to non-existence.

He would fight. He would gobble the pain like macaroons and ask for more. So, cussing and wincing and writhing with each step, he leaned into the bush till it yielded. It was slow going, but each anguished step filled his consciousness completely, leaving no room for notions of past or future. There was not even room for self-awareness; he did not even realize how tough he was being.

Then everything changed. He heard a sound. His heart began to pound rapidly. Could he be imagining it? No! There it was again: human voices, human laughter. He hobbled more quickly, putting weight on his bad ankle and allowing the branches in his path to thrash his face. At last he burst out onto a trail, tumbling into the dirt. But he hardly noticed, intent as he was on the distant voices. Yes, they were coming nearer! He was saved!

He got to his feet, propped himself against a tree, and brushed himself off. Boy, he was a real mess! He picked burrs from his pant legs and dry mud from his sleeves. He ran his fingers through his hair and was appalled to see what fell out. His hands were too filthy to wipe his face with, so he used a large leaf, dampened with saliva, as a washcloth. Then he leaned back against the tree, slung the rifle casually over his shoulder, arranged upon his face a sardonic expression of relief, and waited for the appearance of his saviors.

There were four of them: four rough, dirty, grizzled sportsmen lugging rifles and packs, looking wearied but satisfied, at peace with themselves and at home in the universe. One of them carried an immense pair of antlers, held together, as if for lack of any better adhesive, by a small severed deer's head with glossy black marbles for eyes.

When they noticed Lance, the hunters nodded and grunted their salutations.

Lance nodded and grunted back.

"Any luck, pard?"

Lance chuckled deprecatingly. "None to speak of."

The hunters nodded and grinned, grunted their valedictions, and continued on their way. Lance watched them go, then slumped to the ground and listened to their voices and laughter fade into the distance.

Only when they were too far away to call after did he begin to rationalize his behavior. They had no pack ponies, and he could hardly have asked them to carry him. Besides, he was on the trail now, and could follow it back to civilization. He had water, and he had—a gun.

As he limped in the direction the hunters had gone, he began scanning the woods around him for animals to shoot. But all he spotted were squirrels and birds probably too small to hit, and certainly too small to eat. And since he did not relish the prospect of skinning and gutting his dinner, surely one large fleshy beast would be preferable to several scrawny ones; it would also save bullets. Then he remembered that he did not have a knife, or any means of building a fire. At home he liked his steak well done; could he bring himself to bite into the raw flank of a dead moose, or wolf, or wild boar? He was hungry enough to imagine that he could. Probably uncooked flesh tasted more or less like raw cookie dough ...

This pleasant reverie was interrupted by the sight, far down the trail, of a herd of deer grazing. He threw himself behind a bush and waited for his pulse to return to normal so that he could think. Had they seen him? Had they heard him? Lying on his back, he kicked with his heels and slid on his head a few inches into the trail. They were still grazing peacefully, apparently oblivious. He flopped onto his belly and wriggled back behind cover. Would they smell him? Was he downwind? He stuck a finger in his mouth, then held it out, coated in slobber. Yes; he was lucky: the side nearest the deer grew cool first.

He sat up and looked at the gun in his lap. There did not seem to be any place to put the cartridges, aside from the hole in the barrel. He was about to drop one in, pointy end up, then stopped to wonder what would hold it in place, what would keep it from sliding back out, if he tilted the gun past horizontal? He recalled Maury saying something about chambers—testing the cartridges in the chambers. He tried twisting and bending the gun along different seams. Finally he found a little sliding latch which revealed a bullet-sized trench. He inserted a cartridge; it fit perfectly. Then, with a satisfying series of clicks, like a key turning in a lock, the latch slid back into place. His heart was thumping again, but now with joy.

He peered over the top of the bush. The deer, or whatever they were, had not moved. He could see at least five of them. The closest one was facing his direction. It lifted its head into clear view between bites. He took aim.

His arms were trembling, his breath shallow. It was a beautiful beast, with sleek khaki-colored fur. A shame that it had no antlers. A female, he supposed. He waited for her to raise her head again. She had no idea that her life was in his hands. She did not even know he existed! She was in his possession; he owned her. The thought made him giddy. He could let her live, or destroy her with the twitch of one finger. She lifted her head. He held his breath. His whole body quivered with an intoxicating feeling of power. Then he squeezed, not the trigger, but the entire gun, with both hands and with all his might, as if throttling the deer from a distance. The gun kicked in his hands like a living thing, then was still.

All was still. Nothing moved; nothing had changed. But then, after what felt like minutes, the deer fell sideways into the ferns—dead. He'd got her! He'd killed her! He'd blasted her to bits! His head swam with delight. How much better than literature was life!

He was about to run forward and revel in his kill when he noticed that the other deer still hadn't budged. They stood there, sniffing the air, apparently unable to move, either from fear or confusion. He was marveling at their stupidity when something that Maury had said came back to him. Why, these must be caribou! The very same creatures these mountains had been named for, and which had been decimated by commercial hunters who had single-handedly massacred entire herds, because when you shot at them they froze! Quickly, with his breath catching in his throat, Lance reloaded his rifle.

P-kow! P-kosh! Ch-chow! Bakaw!

One by one, each time with less haste and more skill, he knocked the life out of his prey. The woods reverberated with his shots, then fell silent. Even the birds held their breath. He did not want to stop, but he had killed them all. Five shots, five dead caribou. He was a hunter. He was—

"Are you crazy?"

Maury and the Indians came bounding out of the bush. Lance noticed, behind them, the pale grey canvas of their tents and packs. He had found camp.

"What the hell are you shooting at?"

"I got lost," he started to explain.

Rocky and Old Moose had meanwhile discovered the carcasses, and were praising his marksmanship.

Maury staggered to the nearest one, fell to his knees, and put his hand on its bloody neck. "You shot our *ponies*?"

Lance, still tingling from the kill, refused to acknowledge any mistake. "They—attacked me," he said at last.

Maury's eyes grew wide. "Attacked you? These ponies?"

Lance stood rigid, rifle on shoulder, defying disbelief.

Slowly the amazement drained from Maury's face, leaving behind only a profound melancholy. He shook his head and muttered, "They must have been mad."

THE LANGUAGE BARRIER

SHE STAGGERED THROUGH the narrow streets with her head thrown back and her eyes peeled open, drinking in the strange sights and sounds like a clean page absorbing ink. She paused occasionally to siphon some of these impressions into her notebook, her lips fluttering slightly as she translated her raw perceptions into prose. Each afternoon, back at the *albergo*, she refined and expanded these jottings into long letters home to her husband, which she posted in the mailbox across the street with the gravity of a woman making a deposit at the bank. When she returned home to North Carolina, she intended to mine these letters for material for her next novel. It was to be called *Italy*.

Katherine had been in Italy only two and a half days and already she had collected an incredible assortment of material. She had seen an old woman spitting off a balcony into the hair of an unwitting vendor below. She had seen a boy riding a bicycle that was much too large for him, so that his feet reached the pedals only at their apex. She had seen garbage; never before had she seen so much garbage: in alleyways, in the gutters, in cracks and corners like drifted snow. She had seen little boys pissing in the street—*into* the street, with their backs to a wall. She had seen Coca-Cola served in plastic bags. She had seen very small cats—not kittens, but fully grown cats in miniature. She had seen a dead dog lying undisturbed in the street, strangely black and mummified, as if it had been sun-dried before it could decompose. She had seen a fat man, shirtless but wearing black pants, socks, and shoes, seated on a rocking chair in the middle of a bustling market and apparently asleep. She had seen a man watering a dirt road with a garden hose. She had seen a man in some kind of military uniform holding a rifle under one arm and a baby in the other.

And she had captured all these astonishing things in her notebook, preserving them in noun phrases, as if they were found objects: "That Italians at bus stops crane their necks out into the street to see if the bus is coming." "That in an otherwise empty restaurant, the Italian waitress insists on seating you next to the only other patrons." "That Italian dogs will like *any* face." Truly, Italy was unlike any other country in the world.

And the Italians were unlike any other people in the world. Never had she encountered, never had she imagined such friendliness. Everywhere she went, the locals stared, smiled, waved, or shouted "*buongiorno!*" Hostesses stationed outside restaurants asked when she had last eaten; grocers stuffed her pockets with oranges, for which they charged her a "very special price"; passing taxi drivers hailed *her*, and expressed concern for her feet. One morning a shopkeeper had come running out of his shop to ask her where she was going. Katherine, by making slithering gestures with her arms to suggest peregrination, and carefully mangling one or two sentences that she had memorized from her phrasebook ("Where can I buy a ticket," and "I asked for a room with a bath"), managed to convey to the shopkeeper her happy destinationlessness. The man was scandalized. Taking Katherine's pen and drawing a map on her forearm, he sketched an itinerary which featured the Colosseum, the Vatican, the Pantheon, many famous churches, famous ruins, and famous museums, and which culminated in a visit to the most amazing, most essential, most famous suit factory. How much would Katherine expect to pay for such a tour? Five hundred lire? One thousand lire? Katherine shrugged and nodded in cynical agreement. The shopkeeper slapped this idea out of the air and stamped on it. He took a step closer and said in a confidential tone, "For *you*, my friend—one lira." Katherine was moved almost to tears by gratitude—gratitude which she could express only by purchasing three suits at the factory and tipping her driver 999 lire.

Perhaps fortunately, Katherine had no head for math. The exchange rate between lire and dollars was an awkward enough number (it had a seven in it) to deter her from attempting the calculation. As a consequence, Italian currency, with its funny dour faces printed on childishly colorful bills, seemed to her a sort of play money, which she was amused and titillated to exchange for real products and services. The atmosphere of make-believe was reinforced by the fact that nothing in Italy had a price tag; apparently the vendors just made up the prices as they went along, like children playing General Store. Katherine was careful not to burst their bubble, and paid whatever they asked, with a serious face.

A vendor beckoned and Katherine crossed the street. The old man was selling some kind of green gourd with its top lopped off and a spoon stuck inside. Katherine supposed that she *was* rather hungry. In any case, she had not tried one of these things before; it would make good material.

Holding up one finger, she said, in mellifluous Italian, "One very."

The vendor, who assumed that this yellow-haired tourist was speaking English, heard her say in that language what sounded to his incredulous ears like, "Who knows old train motors?" He decided, after a few seconds of grinding cogitation, that the young foreigner could not possibly be asking for the whereabouts of an antique train engineer, but must be searching for the train station—and someone there who could tell her when the old trains "motored." Perhaps, he thought charitably, English was not the young woman's first language. Speaking slowly, out of consideration but also necessity, the old man gave Katherine, in a simplified version of English, a simplified version of directions to the central train station.

Katherine, who assumed that the old man was speaking Italian, listened with squinting intentness for any of the phrases or words that she had memorized, and eventually pulled from the river of verbiage what sounded to her like the Italian word for "beef." She thanked the vendor sincerely for this recommendation, then pointed at one of the gourds and said, "*Quanto?*"

A light, as bright as that of first love, came into the old vendor's eyes. "You," he cried in English, "speak—Italian!"

Katherine blushed and shrugged and agreed that it was so. "And you," she said, "speak English so well!"

The old man, who assumed now that Katherine was speaking Italian, could not make heads or tails of this statement, and kindly asked her, in Italian, to try again. Katherine, who now assumed that the old man was speaking English, apologized profusely and asked him, in English, to please repeat what he had just said. Then they both shook their heads and turned up their hands and laughed in companionable befuddlement. To seal their new friendship, the vendor gave Katherine a gourd, for which Katherine paid him twenty times its value, and they clasped hands and parted smiling, each pleased to have surmounted however briefly the language barrier.

Katherine walked back in the direction of the *albergo* in a daze of joy. She rapped on lampposts with her knuckles, ruffled children's hair, and stared into passing doorways and alleys like a camera, taking pleasure even in simple parallax—the way her moving perspective caused the various planes of the scene to shift and stretch smoothly and in perfect unison, like a symphony of converging lines. She stopped to preserve this simile in her notebook, and while she did so, her joy slipped furtively away.

When she looked up, she discovered that she was standing in the middle of the street, and that some of the omnipresent honking of horns was directed at her. She waved her arms apologetically, then froze in amazement when she realized that the little black car directly in front of her had not stopped at all, but was steadily creeping towards her. She stared incredulously at the approaching fender, then through the windshield at the shouting and gesticulating driver, then back at the fender. She was flabbergasted. Did the man intend to run her over? Some of her happiness returned on a wave of astonishment. This could never happen in North Carolina!

When the fender was a mere inch from her right knee, Katherine, against her own will, took a step back. The car continued to stalk forward, and soon had swallowed the spot where she had been standing. She became convinced that he really would have run her over—and she resolved this time not to budge, in order to prove it. But again, at the critical moment, she retreated reflexively. It was like trying to hold one's eye open to an approaching finger. She withdrew deject-edly to the sidewalk and the little black car roared through the intersection, blazing its horn in what sounded to Katherine like triumph. Surely he *would have* run her over? She pulled out her notebook—but did not know what to write.

ONE EVENING A WEEK LATER, after she had posted her after-noon's letter, Katherine was sitting alone in a deserted *trat-toria*, waiting for whatever dish she had ordered to arrive, watching the chimney pots across the street change color as the sun set somewhere behind the apartment blocks, and fitfully describing this vision in her notebook, when the English family appeared—being led, with only their partial and conditional submission, to a table.

The Freemantles were the other tourists staying at the *albergo*. Katherine had smiled and said "*buongiorno*" when she passed them in the hallway or saw them in the street, but had otherwise avoided them. Although she would have liked to exchange impressions of the country with other visitors—and though she would have loved to hold an entire conversa-tion in rich, untrammeled English, without having to wave her arms or flap her hands to illustrate her meaning—she was reluctant to ratify her outsider status by socializing with other outsiders. She thought it important for her research that she blend in—that she behave like a local and be treated like one. It seemed to her that her first duty as a local was to snub foreigners.

But when, inevitably, the waitress seated the Freemantles at the adjacent table, Katherine consoled herself with the thought that, after all, everything was potential material, even the experience of being a tourist chatting with other tourists in a strange land. She closed her notebook and said, "Good evening."

Mr. Freemantle, a stooped, wiry man with brown hair and a white beard stained yellow by nicotine, asked what she had been writing; and, perhaps to encourage reciprocal confidences, went on to admit that he was something of a journalist himself—what he called a "photo-journalist." His photography was quite highly regarded in Europe and North America, he assured her, but lately he had found that journalism paid better, so he was focusing on that for the time being. Had she seen the Colosseum yet? He had just written a rather interesting article about it. He regretted that the best parts of Italy were "off limits," to coin a phrase. He would have dearly loved to see the Malabria Waterfalls ... Mrs. Freemantle, a prim, well-groomed woman who spoke quickly and absently as if rehearsing the speech she was about to deliver to a much larger audience, said that Katherine was quite brave to be travelling alone, especially in Italy, especially *now*. But then she supposed one could hardly be surprised by the mess the Italians had made of things when one considered their innate baseness. One could see it in the disgusting way they spat everywhere, the filthy way they scavenged for cigarette butts, the shameless way they inflated their prices for tourists. One could hear it in the very way they talked; she could not imagine an uglier language—unless it was German. She hoped that Katherine was not drinking the water? And the Freemantle boys, giggling and jostling and punching each other brutally, asked for her opinion of something they referred to as the "bogs." The bogs here were something else, weren't they? They did take some getting used to, didn't they? One had to cultivate a knack for them, as it were, or one might miss them altogether. The bogs *inside* the showers were their favorites—such convenience, such sophistication! Gradually it dawned on Katherine that "bog" was British for "toilet."

The next day, Katherine found herself walking through the streets of a different Italy. The taxi drivers now seemed greedy rather than solicitous, the vendors aggressive rather than generous, the garbage pathogenic rather than picturesque. She had the Freemantles to thank for this transformation. Over the course of dinner, she learned that she had been overpaying for everything, that she had been drinking contaminated water, and that, quite possibly, she had been defecating in the wrong basins. She felt foolish, and ashamed—until she reminded herself that this must be the experience of many travellers, and that, therefore, it would make very good, very genuine, very human material.

She was puzzling over how best to present this material in her afternoon's letter home to Jeremy when the first vendor of the day called out to her. She grinned and waved and was about to cross the street when she remembered what the Freemantles had taught her. She frowned, stuffed her hands in her pockets, and walked straight ahead, stiff and resolute even as she passed through the spicy perfume of whatever delicacy the man was grilling. She had not yet had breakfast, and her stomach groaned, but she was determined now to not buy anything offered to her, lest she feel manipulated or taken advantage of. She eventually managed to initiate a transaction, while conforming to this principle, by sneaking up behind a fried bread vendor while he served another customer and shouting "*Quanto!*" in his face when he turned around.

In English blank verse the man said that, for Katherine, the price was only fifty lire. Or perhaps he said fifteen. It didn't matter—for Katherine had fully prepared herself for this moment: She was primed to haggle.

In labored, periphrastic Italian she asked the man if it was not possible that maybe the amount of money being requested for the item was too much money? The vendor said in Italian that the price was more than fair. Katherine tried hard for about ten seconds to remember the Italian word for "What?" Finally she resorted to, "Huh?" The vendor, reverting to English, said, "Is good, the price."

This satisfied Katherine, so she happily gave the man fifty lire and walked away, munching her bread, before he could give her her thirty-five lire change. Only later did she begin to have doubts about her performance. Perhaps she had been wrong to take the vendor at his word. Telling the customer that the price was fair was probably only a formality, a sort of prologue or invitation to further bargaining. Katherine decided she could do better, and sought out a street market in which to practice.

And, in fact, she soon proved herself a worthy adversary in the marketplace. Because she did not know the value of things, or indeed the value of money, she was as difficult to read and as impervious to influence as a novice poker player who does not know the value of her cards; and, like a novice poker player, she was determined to play every hand to the end. Some of the same vendors who had, earlier that week, sold their wares to her for ten times the usual price now found themselves forced to give their products away at one-tenth their actual cost, just to get rid of her. Unfortunately for many of them, Katherine's guard was now up, and she interpreted every gesture of sacrifice or defeat as a clever ruse—and promptly cut her offer in half. Some of the sellers discovered that, for whatever reason, they had so aroused Katherine's suspicion that they could not give away their wares, or even pay her to take them. This unprecedented experience so undermined their confidence in their own merchandise that their sales suffered for a week.

On her way back to the *albergo*, laden with colorful and aromatic goods, she was intercepted by a vivacious man with a moustache like a shoe brush and twinkling green eyes that seemed to move independently of each other. He inundated her with greetings, character references, avowals of affection and undying fidelity, and all manner of offers and invitations, before perceiving her puzzled and apologetic look. Then a change came over him. His brow and chin became furrowed, his expression clouded and brooding, and his posture hunched and diffident. He had switched to English.

"Uhhhhhhhhhh," he said, to hold his place in the conversation until he could dredge up, from the remote parts of his mind, the perfect English greeting, the one salutation that would operate on any English speaker like a magic incantation, like an Open Sesame. "Uhhhhhhhhhh ..." Finally it came to him. "What your name!" he cried.

Katherine told him, and despite the Freemantles' instructions, could not refrain from asking his name in return. Among the syllables of nomenclature that the man proudly recited were what sounded to Katherine like "Giuseppe" and "Carlo." So she called him Giuseppe Carlo, and said that she was pleased to meet him, but that she had to be getting these bags back to her hotel.

Giuseppe Carlo, sensing her imminent departure from her posture rather than her words, blurted out the other magic phrase that he had as a child stored away for just this occasion. "Do you speak English!"

Katherine pointed out that that was what they were doing. Giuseppe Carlo nodded fiercely to indicate his total agreement with what the Signorina Catarina had just said, and even looked around with gallant pugnacity for anyone who might hold a different opinion. Katherine again tried to excuse herself, but Giuseppe Carlo's intense desire that the conversation should continue acted as a sort of gravitational field. Besides, to walk away from someone in the middle of a sentence would be rude. So she shifted the bags she was carrying and tried honestly for a while to decipher what he was telling her; then she gave up and waited for his spiel to be over; then, much later, she went back to trying to understand.

He was, in fact, painstakingly transliterating his standard pickup pitch, word by word. When he did not know the English word, he said the Italian, but with a flat, nasal, "English" intonation, and illustrated each idea with a unique impressionistic hand gesture. Katherine eventually extracted some of his meaning: that he was a good man, that he and she were now friends for life, and that he wanted very much to take her to see the Colosseum, the Vatican, the Pantheon, and many famous churches and popular museums and romantic *trattorie*, which he began to name and translate.

A wave of fatigue washed over her. She suddenly wanted very badly to be back at the *albergo*, relieved of her purchases, out of the sun, and away from this man. "And then you will take me, I suppose, to the famous suit factory?"

Giuseppe Carlo, not understanding, wracked his brain for friendly, obliging, noncommittal words.

"Never mind. And how much will you charge for all this, I wonder? *Quanto?*"

"No!" Giuseppe Carlo shook his head fiercely and slashed his arms through the air in repudiation. "For you, my friend—is treat."

She sighed. Well, the Freemantles were right: The Italians were all con artists. Or, at least, the Italians were like men: the nice ones never talked to you.

"No thank you," she said. "Goodbye."

"But—is treat!" he cried, chasing after her.

"I don't want to go to those places. I have been to those places."

He began naming other places. She shook her head and walked more quickly. They did not have to limit themselves to Rome, he said: his cousin owned a truck. She declined the kind offer. In desperation, he began naming towns and attractions at random, places he had never been, places which were not even in Italy. Suddenly the Signorina stopped.

"Yes?" He clasped his hands together and pressed them to his lips, daring to hope. "We go, we two, to see the Tower of Eiffel?"

"No. Before that. You mentioned the waterfalls."

"The water fall, yes! So beauty! So romance! We go! We go?"

She shook her head sadly, almost pitying him now that she had caught him in a lie. "The waterfalls are closed."

He denied that this was so. He was offended that anyone should be spreading such slanderous untruths about the waterfalls. The waterfalls were a phenomenon of nature, and the beauty and majesty and inspiration of nature were available to everyone, at all times. The waterfalls could not be "closed." It was impossible. It was nonsensical.

This, at least, was what he meant when he said, "No! Not close! Open!"

She shook her head and continued on her way. When he saw that she would not be persuaded, he became angry.

"You stupid!" he called after her.

She turned and stared at him, aghast at his rudeness.

"Very stupid! The water fall..." He allowed a voluptuous gesture to complete his thought. "So stupid!"

He flagged down a taxi and rode away, looking back occasionally and shaking his head with pitying contempt.

She managed to keep from crying until she reached the *albergo*, by which time she no longer felt the need to. She had already begun to see how this ordeal might be transmuted into a rather amusing letter home. Indeed, when she came to write it down, she found that the anecdote required very little finessing. She had to render herself only a little more naive and flustered than she had actually been, and Giuseppe Carlo only a little more flamboyant and ridiculous than he had been in reality. But that, after all, was the novelist's job: to magnify life, without distorting it; in fact, to magnify life *in order not to* distort it—for only the amplified transmission reaches its destination intact.

That evening at dinner, however, she must have told the story wrong, for the Freemantles did not find it amusing. Mr. Freemantle was annoyed that, without even trying, she had found someone to take her to the waterfalls, and even more annoyed that she had, to coin a phrase, "passed up the opportunity." Mrs. Freemantle thought that Katherine should have refused to pay more than five lire for the excursion. It was important not to spoil the locals, or getting a fair price for anything would become impossible. She drew an enigmatic analogy to the feeding of wild animals. And the Freemantle boys were of the opinion that Giuseppe Carlo was a pervert, and took turns demonstrating on each other how best to beat up a guy like that.

The Freemantles were all in agreement on one point, that Katherine needed a chaperone. So the next day they took her to see the Colosseum, the Vatican, the Pantheon, and many famous churches and museums and monuments. The boys read to her descriptions of these attractions from their guide-books, Mrs. Freemantle helped her to purchase postcards of them, and Mr. Freemantle took documentary photographs of her standing in front of them. The Freemantles kept her firmly on the beaten path, where the crowds were. They protected her from touts and vendors and taxi drivers by coldly ignoring everyone. They laughed indulgently at her unnecessary attempts to speak Italian, and showed her how easy it was to order coffee, or anything else, in English: you just shouted "coffee" repeatedly and stood your ground until it was served to you.

Katherine was grateful, as she was for any kindness, but she was also dissatisfied. She had already, she felt, exhausted the Freemantles' peculiarities of appearance, mannerism, and speech in her letters home to Jeremy, and as guides they were showing her nothing new. She also felt guilty; she was afraid of bumping into Giuseppe Carlo, who had offered to take her to these places. In her memory, she, rather than Giuseppe Carlo, had been rude; and in her mind, she kept seeing him riding away in the taxi, looking back at her and shaking his head mournfully. The thought occurred to her that probably he had a large family to feed.

"Filthy, filthy," Mrs. Freemantle was saying. "The way they crouch in the shade like dogs." She let out a sigh like a shudder. "But I suppose one has a right to be filthy."

This was too much for Katherine.

"He's not a dog!" she spluttered. They all looked at her. "And ... I think the language is lovely."

Mr. and Mrs. Freemantle attributed this outburst to sunstroke, and quickly ushered her inside the nearest art museum, while the boys waited outside, splashing in a Bernini fountain with their shirts off. Mrs. Freemantle read aloud to Katherine the biographical and historical information from the placards beside the paintings, pausing to exult in the errors of spelling and grammar in the English text.

After an hour of this, Katherine quietly asked to be taken back to the *albergo*, where she drank a tall glass of water from the tap, then lay in bed, thinking.

The next morning, mistaking the first symptoms of dysentery for remorse, she set out to find Giuseppe Carlo and hire him to take her to the Malabria Waterfalls.

HE DID NOT UNDERSTAND what she wanted. Over the last three days he had taken her to see the Colosseum, the Vatican, the Pantheon, all the most popular churches and museums and monuments, but the Signorina Catarina was not satisfied by the best that Rome had to offer; she was not satisfied by anything. She just shook her head and frowned and delivered one of her harangues in that flat, nasal language of hers, sounding to him like a snoring squirrel. He could not imagine an uglier language—unless it was Spanish. Each time he reassured her, agreeing passionately with everything she said and swearing on his life that the next attraction would be better, but each time she was displeased. After three days of failure he began to wonder if perhaps some little misunderstanding had occurred. What exactly did the Signorina wish to see?

She told him again, and tried to show him: she waggled her fingers and stiffly raised and lowered her arms, like a zombie sprinkling fairy dust. Giuseppe Carlo nodded, slowly and gravely, to indicate his strong desire to understand—and, on a hunch, took the Signorina to see the Pope giving a benediction. She frowned and shook her head and tried again, this time letting her arms go loose and wriggling them in their descent. Giuseppe Carlo nodded slowly—and took her to the most expensive spaghetti restaurant in the city. The Signorina sighed and frowned throughout the meal. She tried again, this time slamming her splayed hands down on an imaginary keyboard and making a noise at the back of her throat like a large crowd's cheers heard from afar. Giuseppe Carlo did not know any popular pianists, so he took her to a burlesque music hall. After the show, he translated and explained to her some of the best, most crude jokes, but she was not to be diverted. She tore a sheet of paper from her notebook and drew on it a picture of a girl with long flowing hair as seen from behind. Giuseppe Carlo, though beginning to enjoy this game, was more perplexed than ever. The Signorina wanted to buy a wig?

Finally Katherine resorted to her phrasebook, which unfortunately had no dictionary or index. So they sat on the edge of a fountain in the center of a cobblestoned *piazza*, and, with their heads nearly touching, while the gulls wheeled in the sky overhead like tourists on mopeds, they read the book from front to back.

In the process, they learned a few things. Katherine learned that Giuseppe Carlo was well, thank you; he learned her phone number. She learned that he liked the weather today; he learned that she spoke only a little Italian. She learned that he was thirty-seven; he that she was thirty-four. She learned that he had two siblings; he that she had none. He learned that she was from America; she that he was from Florence. He learned that her middle name was Florence; she that his was Antonio—or Marcello—or possibly Fernando. She had indigestion; he had a toothache. He was divorced; she was married. (He said that this didn't matter to him. She said, "Huh?") He was a mechanic (when he was not being a guide, presumably); she was a writer. "What write?" he asked eagerly, with the unqualified interest of the aliterate. Like every novelist, she found this a difficult question to answer. She felt like a painter being asked what colors she painted with; she believed that she used the entire palette. Finally she said, "Life—*la vita*"—and for once was grateful for the excuse of the language barrier.

They laughed and asked each other silly, stilted questions about stamps, trains, and passports. Then, on the last page of the book, Katherine found the very phrase she was searching for.

"Why will you not take me to the Malabria Waterfalls?" she asked in Italian.

Giuseppe Carlo clapped his hands, grinned, nodded, and sighed as if hearing his own feelings perfectly expressed by beautiful music. "Ah!" he cried. "Water fall!"

"Yes!"

"Yes! Not possible! Water fall is close!"

"No!" said Katherine. "Not closed! Open! You said so yourself, three days ago."

He nodded and shook his head rhythmically, as if conducting an orchestra with it, and repeated, with complete satisfaction, that that part of the country was indeed temporarily off-limits. "Very danger."

This information, however, did not satisfy the Signorina. She shouted and pointed at him and stamped her feet; then she became very quiet and still—only her chin quivered with resentment. His heart gasped. These American women were so feisty!

"Okay," he said at last, looking into her eyes. "We go."

They could not go immediately, however; the trains were not well at the moment. Their health had not improved by the following day, or the next. Katherine reminded him of his cousin's truck, and he was fulsome in his praise of her memory. The foredoomed search for his cousin, who did not exist outside his imagination, provided the excuse for further delay. In the meantime, Giuseppe Carlo wooed her

savagely, plying her with seven or eight expensive and therefore romantic meals a day. Although the Signorina scrupulously insisted on paying half, he soon ran out of funds, and
finally had to resort to feeding her at home or at the homes
of friends. His shame, however, was allayed by her evident
enjoyment of these visits. He could not understand it, but
she looked around his mother's dirty kitchen like it was the
Sistine Chapel, taking pictures with her eyes and sometimes
with her pen.

His mother explained it to him: Writers write when they
are happy, just as mechanics destroy automobiles when *they*
are happy. "She likes you."

His mother, his brothers, and all his friends were charmed
by Signorina Catarina. They were tickled by her accent and
her childish diction. They marveled at her appetite and used
it to shame their fussy toddlers. And they were positively
mesmerized by her stupidity, which seemed boundless; and,
like visitors to the Grand Canyon, they kept walking up to
its edge and shouting down into it to see if any echo would
emerge.

"What is your favorite color!"

"Do you like tomatoes!"

"What is two plus two!"

She didn't know! Again and again, she smiled and shook
her head and said, "I'm not understand." She was better than
a movie. They sincerely hoped that Giuseppe Carlo would
marry this girl.

For Katherine, however, the novelty of seeing how the
locals lived soon wore off. She was tired of being given
strange new things to eat—including small creatures and
the organs of large ones—and being watched for her reac-
tion. She was tired of being stared at and talked about. The
impression that she was the sole topic of conversation was

strengthened by the fact that, whenever anyone did lapse into English, the comment was invariably about or directed at her. During the rest of their talk—and there were cataracts of it—she could only sit there and try to appear genial and satisfied. At first, out of politeness, she concealed her boredom by operating her utensils with panache or scratching unitchy parts of her body with absorbed assiduity; but eventually she abandoned the pretense, and fell into a wheezing trance, slumped upon her stool like a jellyfish washed up on a rock. Giuseppe Carlo, the only person in the room who might have acted as translator, did not seem to understand the need for one, or the responsibilities of one. Occasionally, seeing her not laughing, he would translate for her the punchline of an elaborate joke ("But the duck, he have no leg") or the conclusion of a long, involved story ("He need his car to be fix") and consider his duty discharged. When she herself said something clever—even if she advertised its cleverness by broadcasting it in a loud clear voice through a smirk—Giuseppe Carlo just smiled doubtfully and kept the comment to himself. She decided that he was immune to English witticism. Indeed, before seeing him in his natural habitat, she had assumed that he was dour and humorless. But when speaking Italian he became unbuttoned: he gasped and whistled and goggled, he waved his arms around like a drowning man signaling for help, he howled with laughter at nearly everything that was said. He was like a boy—a boy on summer holidays, drunk on sugar. She could not have imagined a man, could not have invented a character more different from Jeremy if she had set out expressly to do so. His happiness was contagious at first, but soon became grating. She reminded him about the waterfalls. Perhaps they should be catching their train?

Giuseppe Carlo looked pained, and, for a moment, almost frightened. He promised that yes, tomorrow they would surely go.

THAT IT IS NOT TRUE WHAT they say about trains, planes, and automobiles; they make the world larger, not smaller.

Already, after only twenty minutes on the train, Katherine and Giuseppe Carlo had travelled beyond the parts of Rome that had become familiar to her; and within an hour they had escaped the city altogether. She was almost too excited by the sight of the voluptuously rolling hills, fading to a purple haze in the distance, to enter her new epigram in her notebook—but duty prevailed.

The novelty of the train and the countryside revived her curiosity. Her enthusiasm could not be dimmed even by Giuseppe Carlo's sullen, unsatisfying answers to her questions. She pointed at two men across the aisle drinking a strange brown beverage; Giuseppe Carlo said that it "eased the sleeping envy," which she took to mean that it was tea. She pointed at a crowd enacting some ancient mystical ceremony; Giuseppe Carlo said that it was a "paradise of shopping," which she supposed meant that it was a street market. She pointed at a colorful shrine on the dashboard of a taxi; Giuseppe Carlo said that it "made the air delicious"—in other words, it was an air freshener. She pointed at a group of boys kicking their shoes at a wall; Giuseppe Carlo said, "They kick they shoe." When she saw a man sitting by a pond with a rifle at his side, she did not point. She supposed that Giuseppe Carlo would tell her that the man was fishing.

The train tracks cut through the country like a scalpel, laying open its tender viscera to her gaze. They passed through fields, orchards, and farms, within arm's length of the farmers working on them; they tunneled through hills; they bisected roads at oblique angles; they plunged through the central *piazzas* of small towns, and sometimes through the very walls of buildings. There were no stations; the train stopped and started seemingly at random. At one point, it came to a halt in what appeared to be a large family's living room. Katherine was in the bathroom car at the time (she had spent half the morning there). The window was wide open, and the toilet itself was nothing more than a hole in the floor; she looked down between her legs and could see carpeting between the railroad ties. The family stared at her mutely, with blunted expectation, like people who had been at the zoo too long. Her bowels shriveled. She nodded and waved. Some of the children waved back. Then with a lurch the train pulled out again. The countryside restored her privacy, but half an hour passed before she could relax enough to do what she had come to do—and then the result was dramatic, odious, and alarming. She returned to her seat on shaky legs. She tried to think of herself as the heroine of her novel—*Kelly Newcombe returned to her seat on shaky legs*—but the situation was too ignoble, and too personal, for fiction, or even a letter home to Jeremy. Jeremy did not admit to having bowel movements.

She stumbled and nearly fell in the aisle. A moment passed before she realized that other passengers had been thrown from their seats, that suitcases had fallen from the overhead bins and broken open on the floor, and that the landscape outside had suddenly ceased to glide by. Everyone stuck their heads out the window or climbed down out of the cars to see what the train had hit. After a few seconds of surprised silence, a great chatter of opinion and speculation arose.

"Is truck," Giuseppe Carlo informed her. He spoke with excitement, which she mistook for satisfaction, and scolded him.

"What if someone's hurt!"

"Is empty." His hands flew apart in a gesture of vacuity.

"Then how on earth did the conductor manage to smash into a parked truck?"

Giuseppe Carlo's torso undulated in a massive shrug. "Someone push him," he said, meaning the truck. "And run fast away."

Katherine's face contorted into a mask of incredulity and disapproval.

"Bad people," Giuseppe Carlo theorized. "We ride motor-bus now."

"This would never happen in North Carolina," Katherine muttered—but the thought did not cheer her.

They trudged along a dusty road under a blazing sun for an hour before coming to a town. From the tone and appearance of a conversation that Giuseppe Carlo held with a fat man seated drowsing outside a *trattoria*, Katherine inferred that no bus passed this way. She went inside to get a glass of water, but the place was deserted. She used the toilet anyway, and drank tepid tap water out of her cupped hands. Her stomach made noises like a dying animal, and a great belch worked its way slowly out of her throat like a snake shedding its skin. Her mouth tasted like burnt rubber. She did not feel good.

She went back outside, where the men were now smoking cigars and obviously discussing her. Katherine tried simultaneously to look indifferent and impatient. The local man, sweating apparently without discomfort, looked at her appraisingly, held up an empty glass for her inspection, and asked her a question in Italian.

"Huh?"

"In America," he said slowly, "how much money to wash this glass?"

"To wash one glass? I don't know." She started, or considered starting, to divide the minimum wage in North Carolina by the number of glasses a dish washer could wash in an hour, but it was too hot for math. "I don't know. A dollar," she said carelessly.

The local man whistled through his teeth and shook his head sadly. "So much!"

Katherine did not like the way he was looking at her—as if she were a fat wallet lying on the sidewalk. She began pacing to evade his gaze, while he and Giuseppe Carlo discussed the wonderful, lamentable excesses of America. At one point, a woman appeared in the doorway of the *trattoria* with a baby slung carelessly over one hip, like a bag of newspapers that she was in no hurry to deliver. She took the three of them in with one long, wide-angle glance, then went back inside. Neither of the men paid any attention to her.

Katherine planted herself, arms akimbo, in Giuseppe Carlo's gaze and said, "Okay."

But it was the fat man who clapped his hands together, put on his hat, and said, "*Andiamo*." He distributed coins across the table and stood up. They followed him across the street to a battered truck, Giuseppe Carlo bowing and flinging his arms around in praise of the man's generosity.

"Where?" she asked.

"*La cascata*."

"But surely it's too far." In fact she had no idea how far it was. She had not even bothered to find Malabria on a map; as a psychological novelist she had as little use for maps as she had for politics. She did not even know which direction they had come out of Rome, let alone what distance. "You can't drive us all the way."

The fat man slapped Giuseppe Carlo on the shoulder, guiding him into the cab of the truck, and said that, on the contrary, the waterfalls were near enough to bite. Then he gallantly helped Katherine up onto the uncovered bed of the truck and pointed to a jagged sheet of aluminum siding, whose sun-shielding virtues he extolled.

She grasped his meaning once they were moving and the sun was again beating down on her, but the metal cut her hands so she resorted to hiding her head inside her shirt. This had the added benefit of keeping enough of the dust and exhaust out of her mouth for her to breathe. The road, if it was a road, had been corrugated by past rains and baked and cracked by the sun; she had to grip the side of the truck with one hand at all times in order not to be bucked out. She prayed silently and angrily—but whether for the man to drive faster or to drive slower, she did not specify.

The voice of the driver drifted back to her occasionally. She could not make out the words, but something about his tone made her think of Jeremy. He sounded like he was telling Giuseppe Carlo something for his own good.

The idea of Jeremy speaking to Giuseppe Carlo gave her a shock of dissonance. What would those two ever find to talk about? This trip had made her realize that despite all his worldly airs, Jeremy was decidedly parochial. She, on the other hand, was cosmopolitan and multilingual, could move easily between cultures, and make friends anywhere. When she tried to imagine her husband and her tour guide in a room together, she could only hear arguing. *You shut up*, said Jeremy. *You don't talk now*, said Giuseppe Carlo.

"You don't talk now," said Giuseppe Carlo. He was looking at her through the rear window with an expression that she had never seen on his face, and which seemed as out of place there as a scar. The truck was stopping. She removed the shirt from her face and looked around, blinking and squinting in the dust.

Two men in grey uniforms approached the truck. In the road beyond them was a cluster of grey covered vehicles, where other men in grey caps squatted, some of them smoking, all of them clutching rifles.

"A checkpoint?"

"*Sta' zitto!*" said the fat man through his teeth.

Was it a border? They were in the middle of nowhere. She saw nothing but endless rows of young pear trees supported by wooden stakes, which rolled away across the black fields in perfect formation like gravestones in a military cemetery. A great setting for a chapter in her novel, she decided. But the guns would have to be removed; they were too vulgarly ominous.

The two men in uniform slowly circled the truck, muttering thoughtfully to each other. Then one of them, the shorter one, leaned against the passenger side door and made an observation—at least it did not sound like a question, and neither man inside the truck apparently felt obliged to answer. Then the tall man began making observations which the short one repeated, still without eliciting any reply from Giuseppe Carlo or the driver. The uniformed men's lackadaisical manner struck Katherine as deplorably unprofessional, and she made this opinion public through the angle at which she held her head. She was as urgently conscious of the passport in her bag as of an ace of trumps in an otherwise mediocre hand, but the officials gave her no opportunity to play it. Finally, Giuseppe Carlo and the fat man spoke a few unemphatic sentences, also as if speaking only to each other, and after some more circling and philosophizing the two men in grey backed away from the truck and waved them on, as if dismissing a crackpot theory.

When they were moving again, she asked why they had been stopped, but did not pursue the matter when neither man replied. She had learned that her own impressions were more interesting than Giuseppe Carlo's explanations.

KATHERINE, WHO HAD BEEN to Niagara Falls, was not terribly impressed by the Malabria Waterfalls, which seemed to her more like a long winding water-staircase. She concealed her disappointment, however, from Giuseppe Carlo, whose every hair and muscle trembled with bated triumph, like an athlete or a magician awaiting his audience's thunderous applause.

They dipped their feet in the cool, dirty water, and Katherine washed the sweat and the dust, which the sweat had turned to mud and the sun had cooked to a brittle crust, from her arms and face and neck. Then, for five seconds, they sat, side by side, listening to the trickle of the stream through little corridors of stone, and watching the overlapping coins of sunlight dance across the shivering membrane of shadow cast by the trees; then Giuseppe Carlo turned, and, as if tuning a radio, put his hands on her breasts.

The blood in Katherine's body redistributed itself in strange and uncomfortable concentrations; her head seemed to have too much of it and her heart too little. She staggered to her feet and stood there for a moment, alternately gaping and squeezing her fists, before remembering to slap him. She did this twice, once with each hand, but without any manifest result: Giuseppe Carlo continued to leer at her hopefully, his eyes wide and moist and not quite calibrated. The scene acquired a muffled, drunken quality when she stooped to collect her shoes, a prosaic action which clashed ludicrously with Giuseppe Carlo's assault.

She hurried away, trying to escape her embarrassment and confusion. She had reached the road by the time her emotions cooled enough for thoughts to be precipitated out. What had he been thinking? Had he forgotten she was married? Didn't he care? Had this been his plan all along? Was this the way all Italian tour guides behaved? Did he suppose that *she* was attracted to *him*? Was she?

In any event, she had not come halfway around the world to kiss a man other than her husband. If all she had wanted was an affair, she could have stayed in North Carolina.

But that was not the sort of novel she was interested in writing. She was not that sort of novelist.

A sinking despair, almost like lightheadedness, came over her at the realization that none of this could be salvaged, none of it could ever be converted to fiction. For the second time that day, and the second time in her life, she had undergone an experience that her art could not translate. But if there were things of which art could make no use, of what use was art?

A phantasmagoria of bad, unusable material, a nightmarish procession of illness and obscenity, paraded through her mind. These images percolated into her body as nausea—or perhaps the nausea percolated into her mind in the form of these images. She stumbled off the road into the ditch and was sick in several different ways, all of them spectacular, and all of which will be left to the reader's imagination—for some things, alas, remain unprintable.

Sickness and the sun scoured her mind clean of thought for a long time. When next she looked up, she found that she was no longer alone. Two men in grey caps were standing next to a grey covered truck, asking her questions which they punctuated with thrusts of their rifles.

Kelly Newcombe wiped her mouth and smiled queasily, but with a feeling of relief, almost of deliverance.

She had left her bag behind with Giuseppe Carlo, and so was without money or identification; but, whoever these men were and whatever it was they wanted, she felt confident that their mutual misunderstandings would be instructive, their setbacks fortifying, their struggles ennobling. She felt that she had reentered the territory of the writable.

"I'm sorry, I don't speak Italian," she said in quite passable Italian—which was how the two men knew that she was a liar, and therefore most likely a spy.

THE UNDERGOING

SHE WAS TWENTY-TWO and still a student, was earnest, optimistic, and ambitious, loved good talk but only participated when it stalled, believed in considering issues from every angle, privately respected her parents, laughed like a duck, and had lips that did not cover her teeth, so that she always looked credulous and surprised. He was twenty-three and worked unwillingly at a press-cutting agency, was restless, deprecating, and lazy, believed anything well written, despised his parents (who had money but would give none of it to him), and had a prominent Adam's apple and a gaze that never fell below the horizon. Neither of them had been in love before.

We do not fall in love so much as ski into it. The beginner finds it difficult to proceed slowly, let alone stop, once they are launched—and indeed, in their inexperience, often do not recognize the need for caution. They move so swiftly that hazards which might have deterred them if seen from above soon pass by in a beautiful blur. Battered veterans call this headlong dash "puppy love." It's fun while it lasts.

Within five minutes of meeting, Terence and Madison were exchanging philosophies. It was amazing how alike

141

they were. She wanted to change the world, so saw in his grievances a kindred revolutionary zeal. He was a rebel and a loner, so saw her zeal as the vitriol of a fellow misfit.

"I know exactly what you mean!" he cried. "'Doing your part,' 'pitching in,' 'contributing to society' is not *necessarily* a good. If you don't believe that *society* is good, then it's actually better morally to do nothing."

"I know exactly what you mean!" she cried. "We've got to *remake* society from the ground up, using the new principles, the new morality. It's got to come from the people, and reflect their actual needs."

"Exactly! How much do people actually need? A house, a car, three meals a day? They could get all that in a two-hour workday—but they wouldn't know what to do with their free time. They've never heard of Philosophy or Art. All they know is Boredom and Status. Well, *work* then, if you must— but give that extra money to someone who could use it!"

"Exactly! The future is as near as tomorrow, but we're not going to get anywhere just sitting around philosophizing and navel-gazing. We've got to act, we've got to *work* to bring it about. But try to tell that to *them!*"

"I know!"

"I know!"

Their happiness was suffocating; they had to turn away. For the first time, they noticed their surroundings. It was dusk, the flagstones were wet though neither of them recalled rain, and the trees lining the boulevard were in rampant blossom. They remembered that it was spring, and that the world was a very large place. The street they strolled down was not the usual expedient patchwork of their perceptions, but existed independently of them, seamlessly and luminously, like a scene in a lucid dream. They gazed in awe at Fairyland, and drifted closer together. After several minutes of effervescent silence, she took his arm—firmly, as if afraid he might run away.

"I don't usually hit it off this well with people," he confessed later, when their emotions had ceased to embarrass them so acutely. "In fact, I hate people."

"Me too, I hate people too."

"No you don't. Really? No. You wouldn't have agreed with me so quickly. If you really hated people, you'd have told me I was full of shit and that people are great."

"All right," she said, "you got me. I secretly love people."

"I knew it!"

"I'm a closet philanthrope."

They suppressed their laughter, as they had suppressed their joy, and felt funnier for it, like professional comedians.

Their opinion of "people" played a large part in their progressing entanglement. People, they agreed, were bland, timid, and drearily conventional—everything that Terence and Madison were not. They saw evidence of their own uniqueness everywhere. Other couples were shy and awkward, or else they were tired of each other and hardly spoke. Indeed it seemed probable that no other couple in the world had ever been so honestly interested in each other, so minutely compatible. Other lovers had been goaded by loneliness and duped by their hormones; this alone was real.

They did not use the word "love," for the same reason that they avoided the word "God": they had seen it too often in print. As radicals and innovators, they deplored clichés and waged battle against all things hackneyed. They took nothing for granted, received no wisdom second-hand, but argued every issue out from scratch. Thus, for example, they decided that although a personal, human-sized deity was quite incredible, one could not rule out the possibility of a creative force in nature: something that would have about the same relation to an individual human as one person's hunger or sex drive had to an individual cell in their body—and which could therefore, for all practical purposes, be disregarded. They also concluded that finding the one person on the planet who best suited and complemented you was a mission of extreme importance but astronomical improbability—and that somehow they two, perhaps alone in history, had defied the odds and won the lottery.

The uniqueness of their feelings for each other demanded unique expression. They became of necessity poets, breaking new ground. He told her that everyone wore a different mask for different occasions, or in front of different people; perhaps they weren't strictly speaking masks at all, but aspects of their total personalities. With *her*, he said, he felt for the first time like all his masks were on at once, all the facets of his self active at the same time. She told him that with every other boy, she had felt reluctant to introduce him to her friends or her parents; she wasn't sure what they would think of him, or whether they would like him. With *him*, she said, she felt for the first time that it didn't matter what they thought; she was afraid, on the contrary, that *he* wouldn't like *them*.

He knew exactly what she was talking about. Always they seemed to be saying the same thing, in slightly different words.

They celebrated their singularity by emphasizing it. They made fun—of advertising, Hollywood, ungrammatical signs, Aunt Agony columns, and the way people walked; they deplored—patriotism, drunkenness, television, etiquette, and public transit; and they flouted. They did not give thanks on Thanksgiving Day, and elected to do their remembering on every day of the year but Remembrance Day. They did not tip unless the service was exceptional (it was never exceptional). They only held doors for the downtrodden.

They jaywalked. Sometimes they just stood in the middle of a crosswalk and kissed—making benevolent, edifying gestures at cars that honked.

They would have done more in this line if they could have; but Madison still lived at home, and Terence suffered from roommates. There was no place they could be alone. It was frustrating. How could they show the world to be a repressive, joy-killing place if they could not flout it by having sex?

They had both read and thought a great deal about sex, but neither of them had yet achieved it. They were now eager to rectify their negligence. Of course, they did not use the word "sex." Instead they spoke—or more often wrote, in long, allusive letters to each other—of the "dissolution of ego boundaries" or the "transcendent expression of an absolute sympathy." This lapse into almost mystical circumlocution was not, of course, the result of bashfulness, but of grappling with novelty. What they had in mind was unprecedented. What they were planning was not *sex*, but ecstatic physical and spiritual union.

They discarded several solutions to their problem as tawdry and temporary. What they needed was a room of their own, a place that only they would be allowed to enter, a place where no one could see them if they didn't want to be seen, a place where they could give their thoughts free expression, a still, safe, firm ground from which they could push off, reach out, and act. (They did not use the word "home.")

Terence did not believe that such a place existed—unless one had money; and he wallowed righteously in the indignity of their situation. Madison's bent was more pragmatic. She recalled that rents were cheaper outside the city. But what would they *do* there?, Terence wanted to know. How would they *eat*? Madison added up all their savings (so to speak), liquid assets, and hopes of credit, and concluded that they could survive for five months in the countryside, without having to do anything at all.

Terence's restlessness battled his laziness—and lost. "But *then* what? We'll just be in the same boat again—but with less freeboard."

The answer came to them the next day, at a book shop. They browsed the stock with sad antagonism, like soldiers charged with selecting prisoners to be shot. "Have you read this one?" "Oh God. He's got more love of letters than of language. Have you read this one?" "Oh God. He's like a lion-tamer with his vocabulary. Okay, so you can control them—now what? Have you read this one?" "Oh God. It's a disgrace to the memory of Johannes Gutenberg." There were some books in the shop that they liked, but they avoided discussing these; it would have hurt too much to find their enthusiasm unshared. They also passed over in silence obscure authors, with whose failure they felt a certain solidarity. Instead they restricted their contempt to popular and canonical works, which apparently only they two had the clarity and originality of mind to find flawed. Scornfully they read aloud excerpts from various classics till the proprietor browbeat them from the store.

"I could do better than that," said Terence.

"Heck, *I* could do better than that," said Madison.

These words expanded to fill a hiatus in their conversation as they climbed aboard a bus, flashed their passes with sardonic formality at the driver, and sat as near the back as a group of gobbling adolescents would permit. When they reached their stop, Terence resumed: "You should."

"*We* should."

"Why not?"

"Well, why *not*?"

So they decided to become novelists. In five months they could write a novel each, if not two. Then, even if only one of those four novels became a bestseller, they would still earn enough to live on for another five months—if not a year or two. Soon their names would become known, and they would not need to write so much. They could take holidays; they could travel. Terence confessed that he was dying to see the world, that he was burning to experience life. Madison, in different words, said the same thing: She still had much to learn about the socioeconomic conditions of underprivileged people in other countries. Once equipped with this first-hand knowledge, she would write even better, even more devastatingly persuasive and improving novels. Ever since the advent of Terence in her life, Madison had found school rather—academic. She was tired of endlessly discussing what should be done with the world; it was time to take action; it was time to *tell* people what should be done with the world. Terence knew exactly what she was talking about. Novel-writing appealed to him for the same reasons: it was artistic, it was easy, it was lucrative, and he would be his own boss. He hated bosses. He did not believe in being told what to do. Even in the matter of press-cuttings, he believed in following one's own daemon. He was ready to leave immediately— tomorrow, if possible. He seemed eager to burn as many bridges behind him as possible. His example was exciting, his enthusiasm contagious. So, to prove to her professors, her parents, and her friends the strength of her conviction, Madison dropped out a mere three weeks before graduation. She forgave them their dismay, realizing that guilt and envy had made them defensive of their own safe and stodgy lives.

They packed everything they needed into two suitcases and caught a train south. The world seemed to sit back and stretch its legs as grey tenements and smoking factories gave way to rolling hills and fields in flower; the very birds in the trees seemed to sing tribute to the young couple's courage. They had *escaped*. Terence stuck his head out the window to inhale the fragrance of freedom and received instead a swarm of insects like a fistful of gravel in the face. The pain and embarrassment soon faded, washed away on the wave of their happiness, though the welts lasted several days.

When at last they had reached their destination and found themselves alone in the cabin they had rented by the lake, their triumph was too palpable; it made them giddy. So they walked into town and busied themselves with grocery shopping—"stocking the pantry," they called it. But even this simple domestic ritual seemed on this day freighted with symbolism, charged with an almost erotic significance— which they attempted to defuse with mockery, by parodying the stereotypical male and female. Terence hitched his thumbs on imaginary suspenders, nodded authoritatively, and called Madison "Mother" in a condescending drawl; while she became flustered, hectoring, and house-proud. They kept it up all the way back to the cabin, where she squirreled away their purchases while he lolled patriarchally, muttering advice from an armchair.

The game fizzled out over supper. They ate in silence; their gazes were skittish. Finally they laughed at their shyness and took it firmly in hand.

"Why don't we take off our clothes?," Madison asked in the same practical tone that Terence had once used to suggest they pee behind some bushes in the park.

"Well, why not?"

They did not watch each other undress, but presented a finished nudity, which proved all the more overwhelming.

Terence, trembling, said, "Why don't we have a bath?"

"Why not?"

They studied each other surreptitiously as Madison opened the faucets and Terence attended to the water heater. Terence had seen breasts before, but never so closely or so uninterruptedly. Each time a girl had taken her shirt off in his presence or field of view he had felt towards her breasts the way he'd felt as a child towards other children's birthday presents. Now he felt as if he'd been told that it was really his birthday after all. His internal organs swelled with gratitude. Madison meanwhile was overcome with awe at the casual, indifferent way that Terence flung his naked body about. Her own body was of course insipidly familiar, but it seemed inconceivable that anyone could ever come to take for granted such a strange, hairy, bony miracle of biological engineering as Terence's. His skin next to her bland smoothness seemed amazingly coarse and textured, almost iridescent, like the skin of a lizard.

The bathtub, which was hardly big enough for both of them, overflowed when they squeezed themselves in. The water was freezing; apparently the water heater, though noisily and dangerously lit, did exactly nothing. They climbed out, ran slipping and shivering to the bedroom, and jumped into the bed to get warm.

The rest came easily.

Madison felt as if she were remembering something important, something she had forgotten she had even forgotten. Terence knew that he had found home. He vowed never again to leave—and promptly fell asleep.

TERENCE AWOKE TO PARALYSIS. Something vast, conscious, and malevolent was crouching on his chest, pinning his arms and legs, and sucking the air from his lungs. He struggled, as vainly as an ant crushed beneath a boot. His heart thudded as if intent on escaping this dying body. He shouted, but no sound came. He kicked and flailed, but could not move. It was exactly like a nightmare: he stomped on the brakes, but the road was icy and sloped downhill.

Then it was over. This happened most mornings lately, but he never remembered this at the time, and when the ordeal was over he no longer needed reassurance. Almost instantly he began to forget what it had been like. He was inclined to treat the whole thing as a metaphor. He turned onto his side, and, as usual, found Madison's side of the bed as cold and unrumpled as a reproach. If he felt sometimes like he was being crushed, he knew who was to blame.

He lay in bed a few minutes longer. He was not tired at the moment, but knew he would be soon. He was sleepy all the time these days. No amount of sleep or sleep deprivation seemed to have any effect; but sleeping through sleepiness was easier than fighting it, so he spent as many hours in bed as possible—despite Madison's silent, indirect reproaches.

He supposed that she supposed he had writer's block. But he was far too clever for that. He never faced a blank page directly. Instead of wrestling inelegantly with what words to write, he fenced with the question of whether or not to write at all. There were excellent reasons for waiting. But some people did not understand the concept of gestation. If he was not putting pen to paper, he was nevertheless *writing*. Thinking about what to write and planning how to write it was the biggest part of the work; writing was ninety percent inspiration and ten percent perspiration. Once he had his novel laid out in his mind, he could transcribe it to paper in a week or two. Madison couldn't understand this because she was a hack. She had to think in ink. She used her pen like a walking stick, staggering blindly up the rocky hill of her ideas. He, on the other hand, soared high above his mountain, sketching the most propitious route. A walking stick at this stage would only impede him. And to set out too early, before the map was finished, was foolhardy and counterproductive. He would laugh when Madison encountered a wall or crevasse and was forced to turn back. And *she* supposed that *he* had writer's block!

In fact, Madison supposed no such thing. On the contrary, she assumed, whenever he was not actually in sight, that he was quietly producing in another room. And because her own production felt so slow and so faltering, she assumed that he was effortlessly prolific. She resented and envied and loathed his productivity—but not half as much as she loathed her own constipation. She worked—if you could call it work!—eight to ten hours a day, every day, till her mind became inflamed and allergic to language; and still she had so little to show for her efforts. A thousand words, six hundred fifty words—two hundred words! One day she had actually crossed out more than she had added. This was not work; this was an illness.

She felt that she was the only person in the world not working—probably the only living creature. Her writing table stood under a window, and outside that window there unfolded, for her moral instruction, a daily pageant of industry. Honeybees plied their routes, jackdaws built their nests, ants did with relentless purpose whatever it is that ants do, and next door the neighbors weeded, hoed, mulched, and pruned their perfect garden into perfect order and fruition. Madison and Terence's cabin had a garden too. But theirs had been neglected and gone to seed—hideously, crepitatingly to seed. It was like a single organism now, a leafy, tangled, almost visibly breathing organism, bursting perpetually from the pod of its own rotten carcass. It was a living rebuke; she could not have felt more ashamed of her indolence and neglect if that garden had been her own bruised and starving child. She could not show her face to the neighbors.

That was another reason she envied and resented Terence: he mingled effortlessly with the locals. At least she assumed he did. She had once seen him sprawling naturally over the fence and chatting to the gardeners next door, and she had often seen him strolling lackadaisically in the direction of town; her imagination had filled in the rest of the picture with convincing detail. Terence liked it here. Terence fit in here. She loathed him for that.

But not half as much as she loathed *here*. There was no hot water. Instead of a toilet there was a hole cut in a splintery piece of plywood and a bucket. The electricity was temperamental. The food was strange—the produce sweet and crisp and disconcertingly flavorful—so they subsisted on canned foods or ate at the restaurant in town. She did not trust the water, which tasted funny even after ten minutes of boiling. She knew she was malnourished, if not actually poisoned, because of the strange compensating cravings that came over her; sometimes she just *had* to eat three soft-boiled eggs slathered with corn relish, or a pot of pea and ketchup soup, or a bowl of salted uncooked oatmeal swimming in vinegar.

Then there were the insects. The countryside was infested with insects—and not just the aloof, industrious kind, but intrusive, predatory bugs, bugs with feelers and pincers and poison sacs, bugs too large to kill and too small to see. She was covered with their bites. Every time a breeze or a breath stirred a hair on her skin she slapped and clawed at the spot, but the scurrying, burrowing insect was always too quick for her.

"Look." She rolled up her sleeve and rotated her arm under Terence's eyes like meat on a spit. "Bed bugs."

"They look like mosquito bites."

"They're itchier. And bed bugs bite in a line. See?"

"I don't think two points make a line."

But Madison, who was more mathematical, explained impatiently that *all* you needed to define a line was two points. And in any case, she had seen them: little red-eyed crabs scuttling along the perimeter of the mattress like jingoistic soldiers patrolling a border. When she had exposed them to the light they had stared up at her balefully before disappearing into the seams.

All the wildlife here treated her abominably. The birds would not shut up; they did not sing so much as repeatedly clear their throats, like old men with catarrh. One had even flown in through an open window, squawked and thrashed about in the rafters for a few minutes, then flown back out—a message from the avian mafia, presumably. Squirrels too she discovered made horrific chittering noises to unhinge their enemies, and deer (she had seen a deer outside her window one dawn) stared at her with unmistakable malice as they tore out and chewed grass, as if to say: *This* could be *your head*. Even the dogs and the cats here had gone feral, and evidently recently. They still wore their collars, but with an air of bitter irony, like a bag lady sporting a broken wristwatch or a homeless former millionaire sleeping in his suit jacket. They were gaunt and scarred and dirty, their teats and testicles dangled obscenely, and they looked at Madison with weary resentment as one more thing they could not eat. She might have felt sorry for them if she weren't so afraid of them.

The people she did feel sorry for. They were so friendly they seemed servile—as if everyone in the countryside were angling for a good tip. There were not many cars on the roads, but what drivers there were treated Terence and

Madison, as pedestrians, with the deference one might show a mad bull. Once she had gone into the pharmacy to buy condoms (just another item on the grocery list now) and found the pharmacist drinking a can of soda. When she spoke to him he threw the can, which was far from empty, into a garbage bin—as if he had been caught doing something disreputable, as if anything that might divert any part of his attention from her assistance was disreputable. And whenever she and Terence visited the restaurant, the family who ran the place insisted on seating them at the family's own table, which they vacated with gestures of grateful renunciation—though there were plenty of other tables, and the family had not finished eating, and their table was too big for Terence and Madison, and it certainly did not require seven people to prepare and serve a meal for two. But those who were not engaged in the effort stood at a maximally respectful distance and smiled and nodded with groveling approval at the young couple's every choice, then with hopeful solicitude at their every bite.

She told herself that it was not the locals' fault, any more than in olden times it had been a slave's fault that he called his owner "sir." They were servile because they had been subjugated for so long. Generations of bad food, bad plumbing, bad dentistry, and insects had left them weak, dull-witted, docile, and industrious. They were like poor dumb beasts of burden who didn't even recognize their plight.

Clearly it was the novelist's job to rescue these creatures from the mire. But how was it to be done? She grappled with the problems that beset every didactic novelist. How to praise good and condemn evil while telling a fictional story, which does neither? The easiest way would be to create a mouthpiece character who could do the praising and condemning for her, in forceful soliloquy or Socratic dialogues with doubters. But how could she signal to the reader that these were in fact *her* ideas; how could she persuade the reader to take her mouthpiece seriously? Perhaps by making him likeable? But different readers, surely, found different sorts of characters likeable. She did not want to alienate those who, for example, found politeness, or eloquence, or good looks distasteful; she did not want to alienate anyone. It could not be avoided: she would have to dramatize.

But now the difficulties multiplied. Obviously, the good to be praised and the evil to be condemned must be particularized, must be personified. But once she rendered the good people good and the bad bad it began to seem implausible that the good would ever have let themselves become victims of the bad, who were obviously their inferiors. In order to make her victims believable, it seemed necessary to make them at least ignorant, or fearful, or weak—that is, less than perfectly good. Or she could hope to elicit the reader's compassion by making the hero-victims as frail and innocent and frightened as babes in a darkling wood; but then it became difficult to imagine them fighting their way out from under their oppression. And they had to fight. She couldn't simply give the villain a change of heart, or he would become the sympathetic character, the hero. No, the villain must be blackly and unrepentantly evil, and must in the end receive his comeuppance. That much was certain. But then a still more thorny question arose: Who was the villain? To be specific, who was responsible for the misery and stupidity of rural life? She did not know. But never mind; the personifications were symbolic, not actual. In the end she made her hero an honest overworked farmer who said little but expressed his dissatisfaction through sarcasm, and her villain a slick manipulative lawyer hired by a conglomerate of highway builders to bribe or drive off farmers from their land. She showed he was evil by making him chuckle a lot and lust after the farmer's wife. Nevertheless, she felt that with each page and passing day her thesis was becoming more and more obscured by a fog of dialogue, characterization, and event. She was also bemused by the fact that the lawyer, by buying the farmer off, would seem to be saving him from the wretchedness of country living. In order to get any work done at all, she had to thrust these doubts from her mind—but they were persistent, like affectionate dogs nuzzling the very hand that pushed them away.

Terence, still lying in bed, had a somewhat different idea of the novelist's job. He felt that writing had less to do with the crafting of sentences, the making up of stories, or the imparting of wisdom than with the sampling, the encountering, the undergoing of pure experience. The novelist's job was *to live*. He had to go out into the world as if deciding whether or not to buy it; he had to taste it, sniff it, heft it, palpate it, rub himself up against it, turn it upside down and let its contents wash over him; then, and only then, could he return to his garret sanctum and write about it, exactly as he had perceived it. The novelist experienced life so others would not have to. He was a sort of inverted Jesus figure: instead of dying for humanity, he lived for it. It was therefore his sacred duty to do and feel everything that a human being could possibly do or feel. He could reject no pleasure or pain that came his way, and must seek out all those that did not come his way. He must walk every path, learn every song, love every kind of person that had ever been born. Terence, still lying in bed, did not feel as if he were getting much work done here in the countryside either.

But he refused to feel guilty. It was not his fault that there was nothing to do here. Despite his lassitude—or because of it—he had walked every dusty inch of the village, read every sign, looked into every shop, and spoken to every yokel in a ten-mile radius. From Frederickson at the hotel pub he had learned how to play pinochle; from Eloise the school librarian he had learned finger knitting; Hastington, who had taken over Old Jastvyk's farm, had taught him how to operate a combine harvester; Patchmatt had given him an introduction to the principles of compound pharmacology; Webbing next door had instructed him on the advantages of organic gardening; and Bubbie Katiele at the restaurant had inflicted upon him, in overlapping installments, all six nations and eighty-nine years of her life story. Hours and hours of useless talk! Not one thing Terence could write about! Yet he drank it all in with desperate distaste, like a man dying of thirst guzzling sea water. His boredom drove him first towards the locals, then away from them, sent him careening like a pinball from one tedious lesson or tale to the next. Sometimes the momentum of the repulsion carried him right out of town and into the surrounding fields and woods.

It was the end of summer. Insects clicked and whistled and buzzed in deafening profusion, sounding when he closed his eyes like thousands of ramshackle refrigerators. The brittle yellow grasses held their seed pods out to the wind, which never came. The brown trees creaked like floor joists; their brown leaves shook their heads slowly, No, no, no. The dry earth gave off waves of languorous heat at the exact pulse rate of his own heart. All of nature seemed to be slowly drawing and holding its last fevered breath, before the long lingering death rattle.

He lay down in the tall grass beneath the trees and watched the branches sail across the sky and wondered what it would be like to be dead. Not so bad, he thought, and fell asleep.

MADISON AWOKE TO THE SOUND of screams. She was half out of bed before she realized that it was not the babies screaming, but Terence.

She was about to punch him awake—but he was already quiet. She loosened her fists and lay back down, congratulating herself on her self-control and her compassion. Then she changed her mind, and her forbearance became vicious. She only refrained from pummeling him so that he'd get pummeled worse by his nightmares. This was the third night in a row he'd woken her and the babies (the babies were probably awake and getting ready to bawl any moment now!), and with the ear infections and the teething none of them could afford to lose any more sleep. If he was going to wake them all up without even waking himself, the least he deserved was troubled dreams. Then she felt a pang of conscience and changed her mind again. He was the one to be pitied, after all; they were his nightmares, his screams. And they were not his fault. She decided to stand vigil over his slumber and shake him gently at the first sign of any further distress. But, alas, none came. His face was placid, his body limp and soft. Even as she drifted back to sleep her resentment returned. He made her worry for nothing!

When morning came she found herself in a bad mood, which at first she tried to defuse with physiological explanations. She had not slept; she had not eaten; she needed a coffee. But the line between internal and external causation is a thin one, and soon she was crossing it. *Why*, after all, hadn't she slept? Or eaten? Or had her morning cup of coffee? The answer was not far to seek.

"Sorry," said Terence. "I didn't realize this was the last cup. I'll make some more."

But she didn't want more; she wanted her original share. Was that too much to ask? Then she realized that she was being unreasonable, and tried to withdraw peacefully from the incipient argument by waiving her rights. She'd changed her mind, she said; she didn't want any coffee after all. But Terence saw this as a martyr's pose, and insisted irritably that it was no trouble. He got up and began banging pots and spoons and coffee tin. She did not like being made to feel like a moody, demanding, manipulative prima donna, and ordered him to stop. Terence threw his hands in the air and reeled about the kitchen, slapping the floor with his feet, unable to believe that they could be fighting about something as stupid and petty as who had drunk the "last" cup of coffee. Madison began to explain that that was not what they were arguing about at all, but before she could get the words out she was overwhelmed by insulted indignation. Did he really think she was the sort of bird-brained nag who picked a fight over something as silly as that?

"Why are you *yelling* at me?"

"I'm *not* yelling!" she yelled.

Terence made choking spluttering noises, tried to detach his head from his spinal column, threw his cup of coffee at the wall, and juddered like an unbalanced washing machine across the apartment and out the door—which he took care to slam, so the neighbors would know who the wronged party was.

After this she stopped trying to defuse her bad mood and started instead to fortify and embroider it with justifications. These came readily to mind, in orderly single file, as if they had been waiting in the wings for their cue.

First there was the matter of money. There wasn't enough of it. She could not believe how much more things cost when you were buying for four people; surely something more nefarious than straightforward multiplication was involved. Even well before the arrival of the babies, she and Terence had stopped going out to dinner, movies, or concerts altogether, because she could not accept that the price of these outings should be, for a couple, double what it had been for herself as a single woman.

Terence, of course, refused to worry about finances— which was why she had to; and *that* was why he didn't have to. It wasn't fair. She wasn't parsimonious by nature, and didn't appreciate being cast in the role of tightfisted housewife. She hated what he had made her become. And she didn't find it helpful when he advised her to "relax."

She wasn't allowed to fret about money because she wasn't bringing any in: it wasn't her parents who supported them, but Terence's. But Mr. and Mrs. Loach, she was sure, had never intended to *support* them, only to help them out a little. Anyway no one could seriously expect four people to subsist solely on what the Loaches gave them. When Madison tried to suggest this to Terence he became defensive, and twisting her words, said that if she had such an overpowering lust for luxury she could get a job as easily as he could, more easily, probably—implying by his tone that there was something sordid about being employable. She would almost have considered it, just to get out of the house and away from him and the squalling babies occasionally, if not for her resolute sense of fair play. She was not going to be the only breadwinner, by God. She was not going to support his leisure with her labor. Though he claimed to be working on a novel (the same novel he had been working on for three years?), she no longer considered novel-writing real work, because she knew there was no money in it. Her own novel had been politely rejected by every single publisher she had sent it to. Did Terence think he'd have better luck? If he needed a hobby, let him pursue it in the evenings and weekends like every other responsible father. And would it kill him to mind his own children once in awhile? And what did *he* have to be having nightmares about anyway?

Meanwhile, Terence's rage had passed. It had served its purpose: it had got him out of the house. Consciously and officially, he could only write at home; but in actuality he found it nearly impossible. For one thing, he was easily distracted, and was inclined to blame this on the little sounds his family made. Even when the babies were sleeping, he could (he believed) hear their boisterous breathing in the next room. He certainly could hear Madison flipping the pages of a book—which she did with infuriating irregularity, so he could not even get used to it, as one could with a clock or a dripping faucet. When, from time to time, the apartment did fall silent, the suspense became deafening. He could still *feel* their presence on the other side of the wall; it seeped into his consciousness like a black fog, and made him feel watched and hovered over and judged. He could never forget that he was not alone, and no one, he believed, could write unless he was utterly, absolutely alone. But when Madison did take the babies out for a walk or a doctor's appointment, his relief was so great that all tension left his body; he became too limp to move or even think. He basked bonelessly in the sensation of freedom and possibility that solitude brought, and dreamed of all he would do if only he had more hours like this. Then he would spend the rest of his idyll, however long it might last, regretting that it must end so soon. So that by the time he heard Madison return, cautiously scraping her key in the lock and loudly shushing the babies, he let out a sigh almost of gratitude—for no one likes to wait long to have their pessimism vindicated.

Thus it was only when Terence contrived to get himself expelled from this writer's paradise that his outrage at the injustice and inconvenience became great enough to actually spur him to work. He entered a noisy café or crowded pub and gawped, appalled, at the hardship he had been reduced to—then sat down and began spitefully to write.

He was spiting his parents, who with their paltry allowance had finally chained him to the life of mediocrity and muddle they had always wanted for him. He was spiting Madison's parents, who looked at him as if he had raped their daughter, and who wouldn't even acknowledge their grandchildren until Madison completed her worthless university degree. He was spiting the babies, who smelled bad and made a lot of noise. And he was spiting Madison, who had become the very things she had once mocked: bland, timid, and drearily conventional; flustered, hectoring, and house-proud. She who had once said that the most important thing was to live with intensity and integrity now scolded him for putting leftovers in the fridge before they had cooled sufficiently, and nagged him to get a job. A job!

How had it happened? Who was to blame? Had she lied to him, had he lied to her, had they both lied to themselves? Had everything changed, or had they merely been blind to realities? As his spite modulated gradually into melancholy, his pen began to move more slowly, and he settled into a contemplative, reminiscing rhythm. The novel he was writing was about the countryside.

He remembered their cabin, and the view from the windows of the pastel lake in the morning. He remembered every lane of the town. He remembered the dim shops and the graffiti carved into the legs of their table at the restaurant.

He remembered the wide fields and tangled woods, the farms and the school and the post office in the bakery. He remembered the people, and he remembered, not their clumsy words, but their stories.

Memories are ideas, and ideas are often lovelier than reality, because they are simpler and therefore seem more perfect, like objects bathed in soft moonlight. Memories therefore are often lovelier than the buzzing hubbub of present experience. Terence remembered their life in the countryside, and because his memories were beautiful he believed that they had been happy there. For five wonderful months, at least, they had lived intensely and had loved each other.

Sometimes, as he wrote in that noisy café or that crowded pub, he was jostled; and before he looked up he would finish his sentence with an especially distant and determined air—while vividly imagining the young woman with large eyes who had been watching him all this time and had finally mustered the courage to nudge him and ask him what on earth he was writing about so intently.

By the time Terence returned home several hours later, Madison had gone through countless cycles of anger and pity, blame and forgiveness, self-justification and self-loathing, before arriving at last at a precarious resolution to empathize. Falling in love, she told herself, might be like winning the lottery; but staying in love was more like a weekly paycheck: one had to work for it. The only problem was that whenever she took the trouble to see things from Terence's point of view, she soon realized that he could be doing the same for her—and obviously wasn't. If she was going to put herself in his shoes, he could damn well put himself in hers! And so empathy backfired: because she could understand him, she was unable to understand why he couldn't understand her;

her tolerance made her intolerant of his intolerance. Then she caught herself being intolerant, and cursed herself—and the cycle started all over again.

When he came in, she gritted her teeth and forced herself to be kind. She sat down beside him and touched his hair. "Bad dreams last night?"

He withdrew his head, as if to focus. "Huh?"

"You were shouting again. In your sleep."

He stared past her. "I don't remember," he shrugged at last. "It's too late."

THE PRIZE JURY

THEY PACKED UP their papers and filed from the classroom, as righteously weary as Crusaders exiting a sacked city. Christin, whose novel had been workshopped that night, sobbed for ten minutes in the washroom before joining her classmates at the pub. They all raised their glasses.

"Good discussion tonight," said Ronnie, who had called her prose "pedestrian."

"Some good points made," said Preston, who had described her plot as "turgid" and "derivative."

Glenda, who had used the words "hackneyed," "boring," "stupid," and, most damning of all, "commercial," said she hoped everyone was as gentle when her turn came next week.

Alec noted that Bruiser had seemed a little out of sorts. No one could decide if he had been in a good mood or a bad mood. When Brownhoffer was in a good mood he threw books and chalk brushes at them. When he was put in a bad mood by the worthlessness of their writing, he hit them with his fists. His nickname, however, was affectionate and ironic. He did not hit hard (though he obviously tried to), and his aim was comically poor. Besides, they all admired his passion, and felt guilty before it. As much as they might have felt compelled to, none of *them* had ever punched another novelist in the face for the flaws of her syntax or the poverty of her characterization; Brownhoffer, according to legend, had once bitten a student for using a sans-serif font.

That night, however, he had been strangely quiescent. He was hunched rigidly over his table at the front of the room as if bowed by stomach pains, chewing his lips and muttering sounds of expostulation, and alternately squinting and goggling at the floor, his eyebrows writhing like pinned caterpillars with incredulity. Occasionally—apparently at something one of them said—his head recoiled, his neck became furrowed with chins, his eyes shut involuntarily, and his mouth slewed from side to side in disgust. But he had said little; and faced with his awful browbeating silence, they had striven to outdo one another in the ruthlessness of their criticism.

"What grade did he give you?," Pauline asked.

Christin withdrew from her bag the battered, dog-eared manuscript, which had been neat and immaculate only a week before. On the top page in blue pencil Brownhoffer had inscribed a large "F." This surprised no one, and hardly even distressed Christin: "F" was the only grade Brownhoffer ever gave. But the wide margins were still pristine and unmarked throughout. He had given no feedback whatsoever. This was unsettling indeed.

"What does it mean?"

"He must be in a bad mood."

"He must be ill."

"He must really, *really* have hated it."

"Unless maybe he—liked it?"

They all paused in thought, then simultaneously shook their heads. The idea was too terrible to be borne: that they might have censured with unprecedented violence the one novel that Brownhoffer had actually admired. Over several rounds of drinks they recapitulated their criticisms, and elaborated them, and added to them, and found them to be sound. Unless Bruiser had suffered a stroke, he too must have hated Christin's novel; anyone with any sense would. Reassured, they broke up and staggered, individually and in pairs, home to bed.

All except Christin, who went looking for Brownhoffer.

Though it was raining and near midnight, this was not a foolhardy task. Brownhoffer did not keep office hours, and could be found wandering the campus footpaths, chewing his lips and muttering angrily to himself, at any time of day or night and in any weather. Indeed, he was as ignorant of his surroundings and as indifferent to discomfort as Socrates, and had often been spotted carrying a furled umbrella through thunderstorms and an open one indoors. He was the most familiar figure on campus, an object of fear and pride and ridicule—laughable to freshmen, revered by grad students, and tolerated by faculty. Everyone assumed he was a genius, and kept a respectful distance.

It was therefore with a feeling almost of sacrilege that Christin hailed her professor and chased after him into the botanical gardens. But desperation is the last stage before despair, and she was recklessly desperate.

"I'm sorry to interrupt, Dr. Brownhoffer, but I was hoping I could talk to you about my chapters?"

Brownhoffer, however, was a difficult man to interrupt. Several moments passed before he realized that he was being addressed, and nearly a minute before her words began to infiltrate and displace his own thoughts. He awoke to Christin's presence as gradually and incompletely as a medieval clergyman awakening to theological doubts.

"Yes?" he said at last, as if answering the phone.

"I'm real sorry to interrupt you. I know you're busy—probably working on something completely brilliant."

In fact, Brownhoffer's mind was not, as was generally supposed, occupied with the composition of his long-overdue second novel. It was busy nursing grievances.

He had a veritable garden of these, as lush and various and dark and dripping as the one they now walked through. His latest grievance, the one that had absorbed him that evening and all that week, was held against a former student by the name of April Allen. She had betrayed him by not only successfully publishing her novel, but actually winning for it a nomination for the Hart Winslow Prize—whatever the hell that was. Brownhoffer, in his mind the greatest novelist of his era, had never been nominated for anything. April Allen had mailed him a gloatingly inscribed copy of her book the previous week. Reading it, or ostensibly rereading it, he had found it to be the most crassly commercial of trash—just the sort of thing prize juries ate up. He was appalled that she had learned so little from him, and incensed to discover his name in an unprominent position among a dozen others on the acknowledgements page.

"What exactly is the matter, Miss Shane?"

Christin took a breath. "You didn't like my new chapters."

Brownhoffer barked at the understatement. "No I did not."

"May I ask why?"

"That is your prerogative, surely."

"Well—why?" But as the professor grimly pursed his lips to begin pronouncing the indictment, her nerve failed. "I mean, I did everything you told us to—I *tried* to do everything. I avoided the obvious word. I used the first-person present for immediacy. I made my paragraphs longer and used less punctuation for momentum. I withheld; I mean, gosh, I deleted whole swaths of exposition, really I did. And I read all those books you told us to. Henry James, Proust, *The Human Comedy*—I know I don't read French and I know it's not the same in translation but I *did* read all of it, just like you said we should."

Brownhoffer awoke more fully to Christin, who was the source of a major grievance in her own right. She was by far the most earnest, conscientious, and therefore irritating student in his workshop that year. Of course, all his students were irritating, always; with their questions that could not be answered, their allusions to authors and books he had never heard of, and their referral to him for adjudication of all their esoteric squabbles, they constituted a perpetual threat to his authority and dignity. He defended himself with a pose of sorrowful disdain for their ignorance, and fobbed them off with plausible quotations and impossible homework assignments; but Christin Shane alone among them asked for his sources and completed the assignments.

"You read *all* of Balzac's *Comédie humaine*?"

"Well sure. Over the holidays. And James and Proust and Trollope, like you said. It was real helpful, too. Well," she admitted ashamedly, "Trollope's *Letters* were a bit dull in parts."

Brownhoffer grasped this straw. "That was the entire *point* of the exercise, Miss Shane. Give me your manuscript."

She handed him the disheveled heap of paper.

"Trollope's dullness is legendary. You don't suppose I directed you to him for his lyrical prose? You must know your enemy. Trollope's collected works provide the most estimable education in how *not* to write fiction. I should have thought that was obvious; but I see the lesson was lost on you. Here! on your very first page: 'He held the door open for her.' Period. My God. My God!" He was genuinely angry now; pellucid prose had that effect on him. "I have read that same sentence ten thousand times in my life—*must* I read it again? If you can't say anything new, please, Miss Shane, don't say anything at all."

She hung her head. "I know. I *know*. I *tried* to make that lyrical, but I couldn't see how. There are some things I just don't understand how you're supposed to say them—creatively," she said, for the word "poetically" had been banned from Brownhoffer's classroom. "'He held the door open for her'—I mean, that's what he did. That's all he did. How else do you say it?"

"There are a million and one ways to say it; I could give you fifty off the top of my head. 'His hand lingered on the door to permit her egress.' 'He maintained the portal's agapeness to facilitate her passage.' 'In the doorway he paused, that her progress through the doorway might be unimpeded.'"

Christin shook her head in wretched admiration.

He made a dismissive gesture. "These are not brilliant by any means—but my God! they are a damn sight better than 'He held the door open for her.' Did he now? Did he indeed? Show me! Prove it to me. How did he do it? Describe his hold: Was it firm? Was it hesitating? Describe the door: Was it oaken? Was it glass? Describe the openness of the door: Was it ajar? Was it yawning? Describe him! Describe her! Where are the adjectives, Miss Shane? Adjectives!"

"But Dr. Brownhoffer, the door's not really important, is it?"

"Everything is important!" he screamed, crumpling the sodden manuscript to his chest. "Or nothing is important! *That* is what your writing would have me believe!" His wet face in the green shadows was grotesquely gnarled. "Nothing matters. All is vain. Why live? Why, indeed, go on living, if 'He held the door open for her'?"

Christin was crestfallen. Her novel had made her professor not want to live. She probably deserved her "F." Despair began to trickle through her.

"Maybe I'm just not cut out to be a novelist."

"No one is 'cut out,'" he said, handling her idiom with distaste. "One must labor at writing, endlessly. One must *make oneself* a novelist." He handed back the chapters of her novel and said with a sneer, "You're young yet."

This was the closest that Brownhoffer in thirty-five years of teaching had ever come to positive encouragement; but its effect was lost on Christin, who happened to know that she was already ten years older than Brownhoffer had been when he had published his novel.

They emerged from the gardens. The rain slackened to a fine drizzle. Christin's face, although forever now bereft of hope, became wistful.

"Was it—was it very difficult to write *Gravy Train?*"

What she really longed to ask was whether it had been very wonderful to publish a novel—to package and disseminate across the world a deathless transcription of one's soul.

"Of course it was difficult," said Brownhoffer, his thoughts already reverting to April Allen.

"I thought so," she sighed voluptuously, as if he had answered her unspoken question instead.

But the mention by name of Brownhoffer's novel was too rare an occurrence not to have some effect on him, however belated. His posture became rigid and his expression wary. "You wouldn't have asked that, had you read it."

"I did read it—once," she said. In fact she had read it once in the fall before class started and twice more during the holidays; but she had not understood it at any time, and did not want to risk implying a familiarity or fondness she did not possess.

"When? How? Where did you find a copy?"

"I don't know," she stammered. "Interlibrary loan. From someplace in Texas, I think."

A change came over Brownhoffer. His pace slowed and grew languorous. His eyes became thoughtful and far-seeing, while his mouth became horribly, unnaturally contorted. Though Christin could not have known it, Brownhoffer was smiling.

"Yes, a very difficult book to write," he said complacently, and inaccurately.

Though Brownhoffer did not remember it, the writing of his novel had been a pure joy, for it had been an act of rebellion. He had started with the modest aim of becoming famous, and it had seemed evident, from the orderly succession of innovators that constituted literary history, that the best way to achieve fame was to do something different. So he studied other people's novels and soon discovered certain uniformities among them; these conventions of the form he called limitations, and proceeded methodically to smash them. He did away with plot, and characters, and punctuation, and paragraph breaks, and chapters, and dialogue, and comprehensible diction. As the work progressed, it became more than a bid for fame; it became his own personal war on the mundane. When it was finished, he realized that he had not merely reformed the novel, but destroyed it. His reward, he was sure, would be commensurate with his achievement.

He sent the manuscript in two boxes to a publisher chosen benevolently at random, and for a week confidently awaited the first stunned recognition of his genius. In the weeks that followed, expectation gave way slowly to puzzlement, and puzzlement, painfully, to frustration, and frustration finally to outrage. He sent the book to other publishers; the tone of his cover letters became increasingly belligerent.

It was during these dark days that he refined his aesthetic philosophy, arriving at last at the comforting formula that recognition comes in inverse proportion to quality. The publishing industry—which quickly acquired in his imagination a composite identity, as though all editors everywhere were members of the same board, and had voted against him—the publishing industry catered to the public, and the average moron had no interest in or capacity for great works of art. He was surrounded by morons. Everyone was against him.

Into this darkness there one day came a dim ray of light. One of the university presses that received his manuscript mislaid it; it circulated like a gallstone through several departments before finally landing on the desk of an administrator in Human Resources, who took it for a CV. Impressed by its size and the confident tone of its cover letter, this administrator added it to the stack of applicants for the position of assistant history professor. Brownhoffer's novel, by virtue of its daunting bulk, survived the pre-selection process; he was invited for an interview. He made it clear at the outset of this interview that he had no interest whatsoever in becoming an assistant history professor—a gambit which bemused and beguiled the selection committee. They offered him the job, and because he was broke, he took it. His prospectus, when submitted, revealed that he intended to teach Introduction to Roman Law through the critical dismantling of popular, not necessarily Roman-themed, novels of the present day. The selection committee had second thoughts, and at the last minute foisted Brownhoffer on the English department, which was obliged to give him, as the only "internal applicant," their poetry survey course. When it became apparent midway through his first semester that Brownhoffer was not teaching his students how to read poetry but rather how not to write novels, the course title and calendar description were surreptitiously revised. The dean, however, uneasy about having the college's first-ever Novel Writing class taught by an unpublished novelist, persuaded a friend at a vanity press to expand his operations as far into legitimacy as the printing of five hundred copies of *Gravy Train*. Four hundred of these, deviously miscategorized, made their way unread into university libraries; the remaining hundred were pulped; Brownhoffer himself had never held a copy in his hands.

All Brownhoffer knew was that his genius had finally been recognized by at least one advanced institution of higher learning and one avant-garde publishing house. He had been published; and that put him, not by degree but qualitatively, above his students.

"A difficult book to write," he said, "and a difficult book to read. But worth the effort, I daresay, for those capable of expending it, eh?"

Christin risked a grunt of agreement.

He chuckled conspiratorially. "*You* realize, of course, that great art is seldom—*accessible*. Art, if it *is* art, is transformative; and transformation is never easy. Indeed it is positively unpleasant."

Now Christin nodded readily, for the reading of *Gravy Train* had certainly been that.

Brownhoffer looked at his student more carefully, and was surprised to find on her face lines of intelligence where previously he had found only shrewish pertinacity and impudence. It occurred to him now that these might be the very qualities of his ideal reader. His manner became expansive and benignant.

"Literature is an act of communication—an act of communion, one might even say. Without finely tuned receivers, even the most powerful transmissions go unheard. I am quite fortunate in that my audience, though small, has always been receptive. Of course, all true art finds its proper home eventually. One need not despise one's detractors, for their detraction only proves their unfitness for one's message. The seed does not curse the sand, but goes on seeking the soil."

"But Dr. Brownhoffer," said Christin, after giving this aphorism a respectful pause, "what's the point of revising, then, if everything finds its own audience? Isn't one kind of novel just as good as the next?"

If Christin had asked this question an hour ago, Brownhoffer might have inflicted upon her *A Dance to the Music of Time*; now he laughed indulgently.

"It depends on whether you believe that one kind of audience is as good as the next."

Christin sighed. After six months in Brownhoffer's class, she knew that the only audience worth striving for was the one that Brownhoffer himself represented—and *he* hated her writing.

"Yes," he said, "doubtless there is an audience for everything. There is even an audience for 'He held the door open for her'—probably even a large audience, and one that will pay you handsomely and bedeck you with laurels and literary prizes for giving it prose that skims across the surface of the mind without raising a ripple. If that audience is your ambition, Miss Shane, you may yet have a bright future ahead. But I feel I must be honest with you."

Her face loomed out of the mists in his mind and became almost clear before his eyes. The rain, which he had at no point noticed, had now stopped, but drops still clung to her brow and eyelashes and caught the light from a nearby window like tiny diamonds. A great tenderness welled up within him, both for her, and, at the thought of the kindness he was about to do, for himself.

"If your goal is to be *good*—well. I must tell you that there is no hope. You have worked hard; you have done your best; you are not to blame. There is no crank that you can turn to produce literature. There is no dictionary for translating the obvious phrase into the lyrical one. There is no formula for creativity. One either has the capacity to become an artist, or one does not. You do not. I believe that my candor will save you much heartache in the future. There is no need to thank me. It is the least I can do—for a fan."

And her face faded from his consciousness as he continued on his way, humming tunelessly and munching his lips.

CLINT LEWES APPEARED DISTRESSED. Indeed, he looked like a husband in a Victorian novel awaiting news of a parturition. He paced or sat fidgeting in various twisted postures, chain-smoking cigarettes and plucking non-existent flakes of tobacco from his lips. Occasionally he leapt with sudden resolve across the study to seize some knick-knack or framed photograph, turning it over in his hands with bewilderment and rue. He muttered continuously to himself, but a careful analysis would have revealed that his sentences did not parse. His gaze roved wildly around the room, but there was one object it did not touch; and that was the blank sheet of paper on his writing desk.

He had done everything; there was nothing left to be done. He had retrieved, opened, read twice, and verbosely answered that day's fan mail. He had couriered that week's three and next week's four book reviews to the eleven newspapers publishing them, but had not yet received a new batch of novels to be reviewed. He had long ago mailed out that season's stack of grant applications. He had written thank-you postcards to the facilitators of last year's writers' retreats and registered for next year's. There were four weeks till his next writer-in-residency at the public library, and he had already selected the books and quotations with which he would decorate his office. He had completed the always unpleasant task of editing his latest book, a collection of topical essays. The last literary festival was a month behind him and the next a month away. He had offered himself to a panel discussion on the Future of the Novel that was ostensibly being held at an elementary school in a neighboring province, but had not yet heard back from the organizers, a klatch of ignorant and unprofessional fifth-graders. And he had done all that could be done to promote his most recent novel, including countless interviews for television, radio, and print, and innumerable readings in every kind of venue. He was expected to give one more twenty-minute performance next week at a retirement home, but he had already memorized forty-five minutes of text, complete with the pauses and small charming errors that would make his delivery seem unpracticed, even, in the words of one reviewer, "almost extempore." But otherwise, the invitations to talk about himself, about his influences, and about his work had dried up. They always did, eventually. No one was interested in Clint Lewes anymore. There was nothing else for it but to write another novel.

But what did one write a novel about? Though he had written thirty-seven of them, he had no idea how to go about it. Did one begin with a character? His family and friends were all bone-weary of being cast, more or less undisguised, in his *romans à clef*, and no one else came to mind. Did one begin with a setting? The study of a popular but critically underappreciated—doctor, perhaps? Or did one begin instead with an event, and allow one's setting and characters to take the shape dictated by the exigencies of plot? He clutched at this proposition hungrily, as if he had discovered one of the eternal laws of literature, and looked around the room for events. But nothing moved. He ran to the window and was disgusted to see only two children digging holes in the lot across the street; he had already written a novel about spelunking. He ransacked his past for memories of things that sometimes happened to human beings, but his life and the lives of everyone he knew seemed uncannily devoid of circumstance. The single most common question he was asked by fans and inter-viewers was the one about where his ideas came from; and though he was careful to expunge from his answers all trace of amusement, condescension, or boredom, the question had always struck him as rather stupid. Today, however, he would have paid any price to remember what his answers had been. Where *did* he get his ideas from? Experience? Imagination? Books?

He had torn open the dictionary and was contemplating the dramatic possibilities of the word "partridge" when the telephone rang; he had forgotten to unplug it. He lunged for the receiver as though he would devour it.

"Hello, yes, Clint Lewes speaking, who is calling please, hello?"

It was his agent, Rob Robson. Did Clint happen to know offhand of any out-of-print books that might be reissued? Harbor Mountain were doing a series of Forgotten Classics for their fall list.

Clint did not; but he said, "Yes, certainly, lots—when do you need them by?"

"Oh, no rush."

Rob Robson was an unusually competent and effec-tive agent, but Clint had no way of knowing that, having never had an incompetent one. Besides, he was constitu-tionally incapable of believing that everything possible was being done at all times to keep his name in the public mind. Therefore, Rob's unflappable lack of urgency acted on him like an allergen, throwing his entire body into a state of agitation and near-panic.

"Will tomorrow be soon enough?"

That was how Clint Lewes came to be writing a scholarly introduction to *Gravy Train* when, a month later, Rob Robson called him about the Godskriva Prize.

After a frantic process of sortilege and cross-reference in the university library's stacks, he had seized upon *Gravy Train* as one of the most obscure novels of the century; it was a small step from there to the conclusion that it was one of the most overlooked and underappreciated novels of the century; and from there no step at all to the conviction that he was the man best equipped to rescue it from oblivion and establish it firmly in the canon—while simultaneously establishing Clint Lewes as one of the preeminent literary theorists of his age: the man who had discovered Brownhoffer.

His enthusiasm for this project had suffered a blow when, in the course of clearing the copyright, he had discovered that Brownhoffer was not dead, but teaching creative writing at a seedy community college. There was something disreputable and depressing about living neglected authors, perhaps because there were so many of them. Also, being alive, they were liable to say things that you had not foreseen, things that did not conform to your image of them or to your interpretation of their work; they did not belong utterly to you the way dead authors did. Clint had spoken briefly to Brownhoffer on the phone, and had found him at first suspicious and rude, then pompous and magniloquent. So, for the time being, he abandoned the idea of the critical biography and confined himself to a close exegesis of the novel, written in a tone, simultaneously abusive and self-congratulatory, that would hopefully make readers feel simultaneously stupid and grateful.

Clint was familiar with the Godskriva Prize as the most prestigious of all the literary awards he had never been nominated for. It was bestowed each year on the best novel published in any human language, and brought with it a sum of cash commensurate with its prestige. This year, according to Rob Robson, the Godskriva Collective had announced, or were about to announce, a new prize, to be awarded once only—for the best novel of all time.

Did Clint want to be on the jury?

Clint hesitated; wouldn't his being on the jury disqualify his own novels from being chosen? But he did not hesitate long. The certain prospect of power outweighed the uncertain possibility of recognition, however distinguished. And in some dim recess of his heart, Clint realized that he was not the sort of novelist who won literary prizes. His was an inferior product; that was why he had to spend so much time and effort advertising himself. How he envied men like Brownhoffer!—geniuses who could produce in a vacuum great works of literature that needed no one to publicize or defend them!

Which gave him an idea.

"Okay. I'll do it."

"Great. I'll submit your name to the committee."

"You mean they didn't ask for me?"

"I'm sure they're just waiting to hear you're available."

But this was insufficiently definite for Clint, who immediately launched his own personal campaign for selection. He flew to Oslo and hand-delivered copies of his books to the Godskriva directors; he let it be known, through the medium of his book reviews, that he was underoccupied, widely read, and in a reflective, munificent mood; he took everyone he had ever met out for lunch and casually pumped them for information; he sent telegrams to everyone who had ever written a novel and reminded them how fond he was of their work. His efforts paid off. The members of the jury-selection committee, terrified of committing any unpopular or controversial choice, solicited the opinions of a wide array of consultants; these consultants in turn hired their own consultants, and so on, till nearly every person who had ever written, published, or read a novel had been given a chance to nominate someone they believed likely to vote for the novels they had written, published, or read. Clint, by sheer force of his unrelenting ubiquity, was on several people's lists. His name, with fifty others, was put in a hat; and his, with only eleven others, was pulled out.

TWO HUNDRED NOVELS, all acknowledged classics, were distributed to the jury in advance. They were asked to submit their ten favorites—as well as up to five novels not on the list—as the foundation for further discussion. The organizers, in collating this initial data, were amazed and appalled to discover that none of the jurors' lists overlapped by so much as one title, and that all of them had exercised the option of adding the maximum five books of their own choosing—all except one juror, who ignored the instructions and submitted ten new titles and none from the original longlist. The Godskriva staff scrambled to find translations of all these esoteric works in the ten native languages of the twelve jurors, and when these were not available, scrambled to commission translations into English at least. Finally, a week before the jury was convened, the jurors were supplied with and asked to read all 175 novels on this not very short shortlist.

One did. Ilse Mienemin arrived at the hotel in Oslo bleary-eyed, misanthropic, and a philistine. Instead of attending the reception that evening, she went straight to bed. Next morning when the jury was convened, it seemed to her that everyone knew everyone else's name and that they were all on friendly terms; Ilse, only Ilse, remained on the outside. This feeling of isolation—all too familiar to her from years of sitting alone in rooms writing novels—worsened her mood but strengthened her resolve. She would not agree with anything any of these people had to say. They were not real novelists. A real novelist understood that art required sacrifices; that to write about the world one must be removed from the world; that one could either enjoy life or write about life, but not both; that good work was only produced in the crucible of an unhappy existence; that originality and beauty only developed in isolation. Ilse *chose* to be dead to life, that her work might live forever. Yes; she was a martyr for her art. But then she looked again at the piles of novels littered across the table and around the room and at the fat stack of notes she had taken about them, and she drowned beneath a wave of futility and despair.

Clint suggested that they begin their deliberations. No one objected to his assuming the role of foreman. It seemed natural that one of the three native speakers of English, the *lingua franca* of the jury, should take charge; the confidence with which they spoke lent them an air of authority that the others could not compete with (except perhaps Max Ür, who, to conceal and compensate for his poor understanding of English, which rendered him effectively deaf, launched periodically into impassioned diatribes on the superiority of good literature to bad, the importance of integrity and sincerity in an author, and the supreme value of truth). Of the other two English speakers, neither was interested in leading the discussion; one was insane, and the other drunk.

Buchanan Dewan had, at twenty, and despite the protests of his friends and family, married the prostitute he was in love with. This act made him a social pariah; and his wife, who had married him in order to infiltrate a better, richer class of people, felt that she had been tricked. After five years of intense domestic misery, she took all their money and ran away to the Bahamas, leaving him with nothing but syphilis. That had been forty years ago. To feed himself he had turned to novel-writing, not being suited for any other type of work. Unfortunately, his reputation in literary circles progressed as slowly as the disease, and therefore in inverse proportion to his capacity to enjoy it. He was now in the advanced stages of both senility and fame. He had constructed in his mind a resplendent Fairyland to which he escaped for most hours of the day from the hardships and disappointments of his life. To his admirers he seemed a sort of bodhisattva, giggling and sighing forgivingly as he contemplated the foibles of the universe; in fact, he was playing checkers with elves.

Tiffany Pram had been writing in full spate when she was called to Oslo. After months of struggle and false starts and chewing her pen, she had finally made a breakthrough; the story had taken off, the characters had come to life, and the sentences seemed almost to be writing themselves. Yet she was no mere spectator: every page bore the unique stamp of her intelligence and humanity. She was, every day at her desk, plumbing the profundities of her own genius. This was the best thing she had ever written, the best thing she would ever write. And then she had been torn away from it. From a creative deity presiding over an entire universe, she had suddenly been reduced to a middle-aged woman on an airplane asking three times for extra ice. She was not a dreamer awakening, but a fully waking mind being abducted by a dream. It was drizzling in Oslo, but the fog and the rain-blurred streets felt like symptoms of her own straitened perceptions. The real world was unreal; what was worse, it was trivial. In her novel, every line of dialogue was character-revealing, every action was pregnant with its consequences, every gesture was imbued with symbolical significance; here, outside her novel, there was nothing but small talk, false smiles, and nervous tics. Would she like a porter to help with her bags? Would she like to eat a little something before the reception? Would she like to meet Mr. Buchanan Dewan? She blinked incredulously at the cardboard figures cavorting about her, pelting her with their inane solicitudes like television commercials come horribly to life. She got drunk, and resolved to stay that way till the nightmare was over.

Clint suggested that they begin at the top of the list and work their way down. Was Novel #1 the best novel of all time? After ten seconds of silence, everyone began talking at once. Clint motioned for silence, then granted the floor to Guntur Kunthi Kesukaan, who seemed in greatest need of it: he was holding up both hands and writhing and hopping in place—and anyway had not stopped talking.

Over the next hour, Guntur delivered a moving paean to Novel #1; it was one of his own nominations, written by a friend of his, and translated for the jury into English by himself, so he knew better than anyone its excellence. The story of a poor village that wins the lottery, *The Lottery Pool* follows the villagers' gradual discovery that riches are meaningless if everyone around you is rich too. Only a hobo passing through town is willing to do any work for pay, and, able to set his own prices, soon departs again with the villagers' fortunes, after cutting their lawns, trimming their hedges, and painting their houses but leaving their roads, park, and school in their original state of disrepair. Guntur began his eulogy to this novel in a gracious and grateful mood, welcoming his new friends by flamboyant gestures into the comfortable and spacious sanctum of his tribute. But the momentum of his rhetoric soon carried him past eulogy to apology; he began anticipating criticisms in order to refute them; his tone acquired a shrill and defensive edge. The tale was not at all allegorical or fantastical, he assured them; the novelist had researched lotteries meticulously and had even lived for several months in a small town. Realism was very important to the author; once, needing to describe convincingly the contents of a woman's purse, he had run out into the street and snatched three of them. Several times Guntur used the word "autobiographical" as an unqualified accolade. He also stressed how hard the author had worked at the novel, and how many revisions he had submitted it to; he was a perfectionist, and the result of his perfectionism was, quite simply, perfection. If the other jurors did not agree that this was a perfect novel, they were crazy. If they could not understand the power and beauty of this novel, they could not understand the power and beauty of his country; this novel *was* his country. If they did not like *The Lottery Pool*, they must be racists. If they did not like this book, they did not like *him*. Well, was that it? Did they all hate him? No one spoke. Guntur collapsed sobbing into his seat, vowing to kill himself as soon as the opportunity arose. Clint—who, with the rest of the room, had not understood a word of Guntur's heavily accented speech—thanked him for his conviction and invited responses.

Lun Li Tseng, who genuinely loved every novel she read, said that *The Lottery Pool* was wonderful. Ilse Mienemin said that it was a piece of crap. Ndatti Mbalu agreed, citing its unnecessary length. She herself wrote with great difficulty, never producing more than 250 words a day after eight or ten hours of intense, hand-wringing, hair-pulling effort; consequently she hated long novels. Hiroki Yomo begged to differ: The novel's size was one of its great strengths, allowing the reader not merely to look into it from outside, but to enter and become part of its world. He himself wrote with great facility, never producing fewer than five cinderblock-sized novels a year. He wrote constantly, jotting down notes and composing entire chapters while riding buses or drinking in pubs with friends or waiting in line at grocery stores. He had, that morning while Guntur spoke, written the first five thousand words of what was to be a sweeping satirical epic about an international literary prize jury; his snickers of delight and self-satisfaction had contributed in no small part to the other man's paranoid breakdown.

Blanquita Reverberone de Calle hastened to agree with Hiroki: The length of this novel was very—long; and length in a novel was something that was—a good thing. She had been waiting desperately for some such intelligent but general comment to which she could affix her support, for she was anxious to conceal the fact that she had read none of the novels. For the past month she had been deeply preoccupied by her agent. Arturo certainly had some of the characteristics of an ideal agent: He was madly enthusiastic about her work, and loved unconditionally everything that she wrote. He was also a tireless promoter, inflicting his enthusiasm on everyone he encountered. But he was not successful. In the ten years that she had known him, he had not managed to sell any of her novels to anyone. And as she was his only client, he had been for ten years without income; she let him sleep on her couch. For nine years and eleven months she had attributed his failure to mysterious market forces; but a month ago she had begun to suspect that Arturo was incompetent; a month ago she had met a new agent. Esteban was everything that Arturo was not: impassive, disdainful, and effective. He told her that her novels were not by any means great literature, nor could they pass as potboilers—but that was no reason why they should not be bought and read. To prove his point, he flipped open his phone and made three brief calls, at the end of which he had elicited a three-book contract, an interview on national radio, and an invitation to sit on this jury. However, she had not seen him again since their first meeting. He did not return her calls, nor answer her letters, nor honor his appointments with her. His secretary's secretary explained that he was kept very busy by more important, more lucrative clients. Meanwhile Arturo continued to sleep on her couch and moon about her apartment, rereading her manuscripts and sighing, gasping, and weeping with admiration. She didn't know what to do.

Max Ür cried, "Kunst entsteht wenn Frustration auf Freizeit trifft!"*

Clint thanked him. Did anyone else have anything to add? Buchanan? Tiffany? Konstantina?

Konstantina Kurgev had said nothing thus far, for she did not know exactly how she felt, and she had made a vow to never do or say anything but what she felt. This had originated as an artistic principle, one which she had developed during her first experience working with an editor: How dare anyone tell *her* how to write *her* novels! How could she put her name on the cover if it was in fact the production of a committee? And so on. In this way laziness and touchiness conspired to mask themselves as integrity and honesty. She made no changes to her prose that were not corrections of

---

* "Art is produced when frustration meets leisure."

errors, and even preserved some of the errors as idiosyncrasies. She stopped writing by schedule and instead waited for inspiration to strike—and so stopped writing. This philosophy of zero compromise found a home in her heart and soon spread to every corner of her life. She strove to make her existence a true expression of her deepest, most unique nature. This meant renouncing many things that she found disagreeable, such as baths and vegetables. She slept when she was tired and not when the clock told her to. She demanded money from her mother and their car keys from her mother's boyfriends, and she received these allowances without giving thanks. As an artist she felt exempt from the soul-staining tedium of a job, and she could no more feel gratitude for this dispensation than a plant could feel gratitude for oxygen. Above all, she spoke her mind. But this she found easier to do at home with her mother than with a roomful of strangers. The matter was complicated too by the fact that often she did not know her own mind—or rather, that some parts of her mind often contradicted other parts. She would have loved to leap to her feet and rain excoriations on this novel as a piece of trash and nonsense; equally she would have been pleased to leap to her feet and pour praise upon it as a masterpiece of fearlessness and insight. But in fact she was ambivalent. She liked the story but didn't care for the prose, was charmed by some of the characters but repelled by others, loved especially the beginning but thought the end dragged on. She could hardly leap to her feet to say all that. So she shrugged, scowled, and said nothing.

It was now nearly lunchtime. Clint decided to call a vote, reflecting that at this rate they would require three months to complete their deliberations. They had been given three days.

He was even more alarmed when the vote was close. Not counting Max, who had voted both ways, *The Lottery Pool* escaped being precipitately named the best novel of all time by a single abstention. He realized that he must be more careful in the future to withhold all power of choice from the others until the options had been whittled down to a few finalists—which few must naturally include Brownhoffer. In the meantime, the frustrations of democracy vented themselves, as they usually do, not on those who had voted poorly, but on those who had not voted at all. Who had abstained, he demanded, and why?

"Don't look at me, chum," said the telephone technician.

István Bakic had not voted because he was not in the room; indeed, he was not in Norway. His exit visa had been denied at the last minute, without explanation. Consequently he had subjected his conscience to a minute probing, which inevitably turned up several peccadilloes. He had burned most of his library and denounced his mother-in-law to the secret police before it occurred to him that perhaps his government objected not to him but to the Godskriva Prize. To be sure, the novels he had submitted were all on the national approved reading list, but perhaps the Ministry of Arts and Culture resented the implication that there could be any higher authority than themselves, let alone a foreign one. In any case, he had received no official prohibition to participate, so he supposed he was obliged to see it through, if only to save face. He had already told all the poets, novelists, playwrights, journalists, and bartenders in the city that he was travelling to Norway to sit on the Godskriva jury; now he had to tell them that the Godskriva Collective, as a special favor to his renown and to his ulcer, had permitted him, alone among the jurors, to take part by telephone. Luckily the prestige of an international telephone call was on par with that of international air travel, both being equally rare. He arranged for the call to be put through to him at

The Punctilious Goose, haunt of the capital's literati and purveyor of the capital's most popular imitation stew.

Despite his many hours of promotion for the event, István was astounded by the turnout on the day of the call. In addition to the expected writers and reporters, there were government spies angling for promotion, bored clerks hungry for entertainment, displaced peasants who had never seen a telephone, and the usual prostitutes and hawkers and beggar children drawn by any crowd. Altogether a festive, almost carnival atmosphere prevailed, which István did not think consonant with the dignity of the occasion. Five minutes before the scheduled phone call, he exited discreetly, re-entered majestically, and made an admonitory speech to the assembly about the delicateness of the telephonic mechanism. A reverent silence fell; even the pickpockets were still. At five minutes past the hour, the telephone rang, loud as a church bell in the cramped and tense room.

"Hello please, István Bakic speaking here, who is it there thank you?"

Not at all deterred by István's use of English, the caller replied in his own rich, demotic native tongue, "Does your sandwiches have pickles? My missus don't eat pickles."

István told the caller to get off the line.

It was nearly two hours before the phone rang again, by which time excitement had replaced reverence and restlessness had succeeded excitement. István hissed for silence.

"Hello please, István Bakic speaking... Hello?... Hello?... Hello!... Hello... Hello?... Hello... Hello?... Hello!... Hello?... Hello?... Hello!... Hello!... Hello please... Hello... Hello... Hello."

By his fifteenth or twentieth repetition of this powerful English word, István began to feel that the dignity of the occasion had been compromised. But he did not know what else to do. The line was not completely dead: occasionally from out of the tides of static there came ghostly knocks and taps, or tinny muffled sounds that might once have been voices. He dared not hang up; they might not call back. Meanwhile his audience began to fidget. In his consternation he shouted at them to shut up, their racket was interfering with the transmission waves. His old friend Janusz stood and explained softly and with greater tact that, though their national telephone was technologically superior to its foreign counterpart, a telephone connection was only as strong as its weakest link; he thanked them for their patience. Nevertheless, several people rose, muttering, and began shuffling towards the door.

"Wait!" he cried. The receiver, pressed deep into his face, had come to life.

"Hello, István, are you there?"

It was Clint Lewes. István shook the telephone over his head triumphantly; the deserters returned muttering to their seats.

"Perhaps you could help all of us here in Oslo out, István, by saying a few words about what you thought of *The Lottery Pool.*"

"But of course, Clint. My pleasure."

It was the moment for which he had prepared so many times in his imagination. He cleared his throat, tweaked his posture, and embarked on an eloquent and largely grammatical speech, adaptable to most of the books on the shortlist, about why this novel was sadly inferior to many, if not most, and indeed perhaps all novels produced in his homeland over the past forty years since the Tremendous Revolution. When he was finished, the room exploded into applause which was, aside from that of the government spies, spontaneous and heartfelt.

"István? Hello István, are you there? I'm afraid you were cutting out rather a lot. Do you mind saying that again?"

By the third repetition, István began to feel that his lecture had lost its freshness; by the sixth, that it had lost its fluency: he could not complete a sentence without making sure that it had been received. By the ninth repetition, he was stuttering plaintively into a void. Eventually the telephone technician came on the line to inform him that the jury had adjourned.

The next morning he tried a new tack: he pretended that the connection was fixed. He spent the day with a serious, thoughtful, judicious look on his face, which he occasionally seasoned with nods and grunts and isolated phrases of grudging agreement or considered disagreement. Unfortunately, this performance proved less entertaining than his humiliation of the day before, and his audience began to melt away. To hold those who remained he began to shout and wave his arms and kick his legs and call his imaginary interlocutors anti-revolutionary swine.

Nevertheless, by the third morning only a few of his novelist friends, one extremely discouraged spy, and the resident alcoholics remained at The Punctilious Goose. István abandoned all pretense of dignity and sprawled across a corner table, the telephone receiver jammed between his shoulder and ear, drinking, chain-smoking, eating cold stew with his fingers, picking crusts from his free ear, and wallowing in his degradation. He overheard brief fragments of the jury's deliberations but saw no point in contributing, now cynically certain of being cut off whenever he spoke.

"... And beside of this, Loach is not a nice person."

"He's an asshole, you mean."

"Yes, just so: an ass hole. He leaves his wife and two children alone and ran away with someone else."

"Please! The author's character flaws have no bearing on the value of his novels."

"*I* disagree. In this case, the strong morality of the novel is totally weakened by the novelist's own immoral life. I call that 'hypocrisy.'"

"On the contrary, it is all the more impressive an achievement! He has, in his work, surmounted his own limitations. Like all good art, this novel transcends its authorship."

"*I* heard that he has narcolepsy. It must be difficult to write with narcolepsy..."

"... Wait, wait, wait. I think the Nazis were not nice persons. Are you saying that the Nazis *were* nice persons?"

"I just think she is not fair to the Nazis. By making them all villains, she comes dangerously close to taking sides—to propaganda. Art should be neutral. Art should not be political. Art should exist for art's sake."

"But, my God! If you lived during the war, and witnessed the atrocities that she must have witnessed—!"

"Excuse me. I believe Cottan was born much after the war."

"Never mind. We agreed biography is not relevant..."

"... Große Bücher verkaufen sich wie Gymnastikmitgliedschaften im Januar!..."*

"... What I do not like is that Gawfler *tells* us how Lord Newbotham changes. This is not good writing. Good writing is to *show* us how Lord Newbotham changes."

"That is a large piece of nonsense. One of the wonderful abilities of the novelist is to *tell* stories. Telling and showing are not different; telling is only showing more quick. If you want to be shown everything, word by word, motion by motion, you should go to films."

---

* "Big books sell like gym memberships in January."

"Well, some novelists could learn much from screenplays, I think."

"On the counter hand, novelists must learn from screenplays how to *not* write novels. The same as photography confiscated realism from painting, movies should have now confiscated description away from novels. But look at this: five pages to describe the face of Lord Newbotham!"

"Excuse me. Gawfler I think was writing before the time when movies were invented."

"That's his tough luck. Art progresses, like science…"

"… István? Hello, István, are you there?"

Clint spoke rapidly. They were out of time. They needed his vote. They had narrowed the finalists down to two.

István roused himself from his stupor and looked around. His friends had left; the drunks were passed out. To what he was about to say there would be only one witness: a thin, hawklike man who sat on the far side of the room and appeared to be absorbed in cleaning his fingernails with a fork.

A spasm of petulant disgust shook the novelist. Only he had been denied permission by his government to fly to Oslo. Only he had been ostracized and muzzled by a faulty telephone connection—for which, he now had no doubt, the local technology was to blame. Only he had been humiliated in front of his neighbors, his colleagues, and his friends. None of this had happened to the other jurors; none of this could have happened anywhere but in the Land of the Tremendous Revolution.

Clint took a deep breath, and summoned all the hysterical superlatives with which twenty years of blurb-writing had equipped him. Did István vote for Brownhoffer's *Gravy Train*—a fiercely intelligent, vastly unique, inexorably complex, tragically beautiful masterpiece; a truly *novel*

novel, a work of jaw-dropping intensity and spine-tingling genius, a triumph of the human spirit, a stirring dissection and fearless glorification of the ineluctable mystery and inestimable strangeness of existence by a shrewd observer of the psyche and astute physician of the soul operating at the very pinnacle of his powers? Or did István vote for Zoltán Szatt's *Pig*?

Zoltán Szatt was the most popular and beloved novelist of István's country, and *Pig* his most popular and beloved novel. Clint had selected Szatt as Brownhoffer's rival because none of the other jurors had seemed to feel at all strongly about him. But the results of the final vote had surprised and horrified him. Not counting Max, who voted both ways, the results were five against five. While it was true that none of the opposing five were particularly fond of *Pig*, they were united in their hatred of *Gravy Train*, and were tired of Clint having his way.

Clint urged, indeed pleaded with István to set aside all patriotic considerations and choose the novel most deserving of the prize by artistic merit alone. This plea was unnecessary. István staggered to his feet and gripped the receiver like a microphone. The spy put down his fork.

THE OLD MAN SAT DEEP in the gloom of the restaurant, hunched rigidly over the table, chewing his lips and muttering sounds of expostulation. The waitress, after contemplating him for a minute, crossed the room to check that his cups, cruets, shakers, and dispensers were still filled. She frowned at their untouched state.

"You got to eat, Mr. Brolly, or that big old brain'll shrivel up like a pea in the sun."

Her voice, warm and solicitous, stirred him subconsciously and set his teeth on edge, like a dentist's drill heard through a wall. He became aware of a bowl of soup on the table under his face.

"What is this? I didn't order this!" He put his finger in it, and grimaced in satisfied pessimism. "And it's cold! Bring me something hot!" He pushed the bowl off the table with his elbow; it shattered on the floor, sending soup and noodles everywhere.

The waitress sighed and glanced humorously at the interviewer, who sat at the next table, out of harm's way. "He'll realize he's hungry by about bowl number three," she said, and went to fetch a mop.

The interviewer shuffled her notes. "Do you mind if I ask you a few questions now?"

"Go away! I don't give interviews."

"Well, maybe we could start there. Why don't you do interviews anymore?"

"If I answered that, I'd be giving you an interview, wouldn't I? Go away."

The interviewer did not go away, but was silent for a minute, having noticed that if she did not speak or move the old man tended to forget her presence. She could not go away: her editor had made it clear that one more failure would mean termination. She had already been fired from every other newspaper and most of the magazines in town, because she was constitutionally incapable of handing in a story shorter than forty thousand words. Although the old man was notorious for not talking to the press, her editor believed he would talk to her—for she had once been his student.

"Excuse me, Mr. Brownhoffer?" A young man clutching a notepad approached the table diffidently, driven forward by a group of gesticulating friends. "You are Mr. Brownhoffer, aren't you?"

"No."

The young man laughed at this joke and relaxed a little. "I just wanted to tell you what a really huge fan I am—I mean, what a really great book it is, your book. I read it three times and it's just really—great." He giggled nervously and stamped his foot to drive away ineloquence. "I mean, I read a lot of novels and yours is just really—the best. I know everybody says that, but what I mean is, I think it's something completely new. It's not just another novel. It's a whole new kind of novel. What you've done is given new life to the novel. You've resurrected the novel is what I mean to say, and could I have your autograph?"

"No."

He laughed gratefully at the old man's disarming sense of humor. Then he darted forward, placed the pen and pad on the table, and darted back, as if feeding a skittish animal.

Grumbling, his eyes shutting involuntarily and his mouth slewing from side to side in disgust, Brownhoffer picked up the pen and scribbled:

GO AWAY

AND LEAVE ME ALONE

YOU FOOLS

Then he threw down the pen, lurched to his feet, and stumbled out of the restaurant. The waitress, tsk-tsking indulgently, watched him go. The young man's friends came forward to see what the famous novelist had written, and to admire his wit and his penmanship.

"Too bad he didn't sign his name, though."

"No no, that's what makes it valuable."

Christin left some money for the soup and broken bowl and hurried after her former professor. She caught up quickly, for as soon as he was outside Brownhoffer was again seized and slowed by his thoughts, as if by quicksand.

"You used to feel differently about your fans," she said.

"My fans used not to be idiots."

"You told me once," she said, "that every work of art finds its own proper audience."

"Who *are* you?" He peered at her closely, and slowly and imperfectly recognized the lines of pertinacity and intelligence on her face. "Why—April Allen!"

"Christin Shane."

"Why—Christin Shane! Yes, you were one of the good ones," he said, taking her sadly by the arm.

Christin laughed bitterly. "Not good enough, as you can see."

"A real spitfire, I recall," he chuckled, handling his memories with sentimental self-pity, like an aging actor mooning over his old headshots. "All of Trollope!" He sighed, then chided, "Why haven't I seen your name on the bestseller lists?"

"Because I took your advice, Professor. I gave up writing novels. Now I do this. Ask questions like," she rummaged facetiously through her notes, "How has fame affected your writing habits?"

He made a sound as if preparatory to spitting. "Fame is when a lot of fools are interested in you because a lot of fools are interested in you. Why did you stop writing novels?"

"You told me to."

"Nonsense. You were one of the good ones."

Her hands were shaking; she stuffed them in her pockets. "You told me that I would never be good. You told me there was no hope. Those were your exact words."

He brushed this aside with a casual gesture, dropping her arm. "I was in a bad mood. You mustn't take such things to heart, or you'll never be a first-class novelist. Novel-writing is primarily hewing your own path, no matter what anyone else thinks of it. No, I remember your work quite vividly. 'He

held the door open for her'—eh? Not bad, that. Quite—*different.* The world needs more of that sort of thing just now.
An antidote to all the foul, obnoxious, idiotic trash being
produced."

Was it possible? Ten years of her life wasted! How much
she could have written in ten years! She should never have
listened to him. But then, why was she listening to him now?
What did he know, anyway? On the other hand, what did
anyone know? Despair, like a hand laid upon her mouth,
threatened to suffocate her. Desperately she clung to the
immediate task, to her role as interviewer.

"Do you read a lot of contemporary fiction?"

"I read the bestseller lists. That's enough. Ugh!"

"Who *do* you read? Who are your influences? Do you
miss teaching? What are you working on now? What time of
day do you—"

But she had lost him. His mind had returned to its teth-
ering post, and was slowly wrapping itself around its grievances: that no one understood his work, and he was damned
if he was going to explain it to them; that recognition had
come too late to do him any good, and now he had nothing
left to say; that perhaps he had not said what he had wanted
to say after all, or done what he had intended to do, and
there was no one capable of continuing, or of correcting, the
work he had started; that he was the greatest novelist of all
time and still they served him cold soup.

Then, after a minute of angry muttering, a pleasant
thought occurred to him. His deep, melancholy eyes for a
moment almost twinkled. He again took her arm, and led
her in the direction he believed his hotel lay. It was nearly
time to burn the day's mail.

ABOUT THE AUTHOR

C. P. Boyko lives and writes in Vancouver.